DECEIVING THE CORSAIR

The crew of the pirate ship the *Lovesick Fool* are worried about their navigator, Sentorr. He's obsessed with working, spending all his time on the bridge. It's not work the big blue alien is truly obsessed with, though.

It's a female.

Sentorr's convinced that Zoey, a female navigator on another pirate ship, is his mate. She won't show him her face, though, or agree to meet him. She's happy to have steamy, late-night conversations with him over comm channels, though.

He's determined to find her and claim her, no matter what it takes. But when he does locate her and discovers that she's been lying to him about who - and what - she is, will he still love her?

Or is the fact that Zoey's human too much for this blue-skinned male?

DECEIVING THE CORSAIR

RUBY DIXON

WWW.RUBYDIXON.COM

Photo by: Sara Eirew Photographer

Cover by: Kati Wilde

Edits by: Aquila Editing

❀ Created with Vellum

SENTORR

"*P*eople...really eat this stuff?" Fran looks over at Kivian, an expression of horror and dismay on her face.

"Like...voluntarily?" Cat stares at the jar on the table in the mess hall.

"What does it look like?" Iris asks, her fingers twined in Alyvos's. She's seated directly in front of the jar in question, her expression curious. She doesn't see the horror on the faces of the other two humans, her radar-sensing visor only allowing shapes and movement, not facial expressions.

Our captain, Kivian, just twitches with amusement. Tarekh looks like he's about to bust his gut holding back his laughter, and Alyvos just rubs his thumb against Iris's hand, his other protectively resting on her shoulder.

The mess hall of the *Lovesick Fool* is noisy this evening. I lean against the doorway, watching as the three human females sit around the table, Cat and Fran watching the large jar closely. Me, I've seen that sort of thing before. It's not the first time the *Fool's* delivered inukni worms to the Outer Rim and it won't be the last.

First time for all the humans on board, though.

"Looks like earthworms with beetle heads," Cat says in a horrified whisper. "Except as big as a ruler."

"The trick's getting 'em down the throat, I hear," Kivian tells the humans, amused. "The skin's really soft. If you accidentally bite into it, it dies with a gush of fluid and then you just have to start all over again."

Cat gags. Tarekh chortles.

I just roll my eyes. Once upon a time, we used to be a pirate ship. We were four males and took our jobs fairly seriously. We never sat around and watched humans just to see their squeamish reactions to settler foods. But it seems like work is only half as interesting as it used to be to the others in the crew. Now they'd much rather spend their free time with their human mates instead of plotting out new jobs to fill our time. Whenever I complain, Kivian just says they're in a "honey-moon" period and they'll settle in to work soon enough, but as the months pass, I keep waiting.

And waiting.

The humans have changed everything, and I'm not entirely sure if I like it. I like the humans well enough. It's the change I'm not a fan of. But then again, I've never been a fan of changes, or surprises, or anything of that sort. I like life orderly and expected.

"People eat them...whole? Is that why they're banned?" Iris asks in a soft voice. "Are they toxic?"

"They're nasty," Cat adds, her eyes wide with fascination. Her cheek is almost pressed to the top of the table as she tilts her head, trying to make sense of the squirming mass in the jar.

"People eat them because they're starving," I say sourly, chiming in for the first time. "Some of the outer farm worlds have bad years when the locals have to choose between selling their crops and eating them. They're so far out that it's cost-prohibitive to get food supplies sent out for an entire family. So they swallow inukni worms. It tricks the body into thinking that it doesn't need food. The bigger the worm, the longer you can last. Cheaper than having food shipped, and it's easier to work when you're not aware of how hungry you are."

They all turn and stare at me. Fran looks sad, while Cat looks thoughtful. Kivian's expression is knowing, and it's because he's known me the longest out of all of them. He knows I'm very familiar with poor Outer Rim farms and their methods to make food stretch.

"They're illegal," Tarekh finally says, his humor dying as he reaches out and turns the jar, pointing at the pincer-like head, "because these are parasitic. If not properly disposed of, they can infest livestock, and the last thing a farmer wants is an entire herd of meat-stock that won't eat. Also, when you unhook your worm, it has to be done carefully or the mandibles will tear holes in the intestine. Easy to get an infection and die. Happens a lot more than it should."

"Not a lot of doctors out on Outer Rim worlds, either," I add. "But people do what they must to survive."

"So why are we doing this?" Iris asks, shaking her head.

"Because it's a job and that's what we're paid to do." Kivian shrugs and reaches out to play with a lock of Fran's dark hair. "We don't force 'em down anyone's throat. We just make them available to those that pay us. Like Sentorr said, sometimes the illegal option's the only one you have. Most folks would rather eat a worm than starve."

"I'm about fifty-fifty myself after looking at these things," Cat says, shoving the jar away with a shudder. "Nice of them to leave us a few as a thank you."

"More like a no thank you," Fran murmurs. She gets up from her chair and moves into Kivian's lap, and he puts his arms around her waist, holding her close. "I'm ready to be running guns again, and I never thought I'd say that."

He just grins up at her, expression both amused and adoring.

Tarekh pulls the jar toward him, pretending to look at it thoughtfully. "Oh, I don't know. I bet if you cut these up and fry them in a pan, they'd make decent eating."

"That's because you'll eat anything," Cat tells him, wrinkling her nose. "I swear your stomach's as big as that flapping mouth of yours."

"You had no complaints about my eating skills last night," he says, and she launches herself across the mess to cover his mouth with her hand while the others erupt into laughter. Alyvos—fighting, always ready for battle Alyvos—just shakes his head with amusement at their antics and presses his mouth to the back of Iris's hand.

Keffing sad that this is a pirate crew. I bite back my disgust. I'm not mad at them. I'm not mad that they're in love with their mates. It's just a mixture of frustration over the changes going on in the *Fool's* crew, bad memories from the inukni worms, and maybe my own loneliness pouring through. Either way, I'm bad company. I push off the wall. "I'm heading to the bridge. I'll take the night shift."

No one says anything. I've taken the night shift a lot lately, ever since Iris came on board and all of the others were officially paired up. I don't mind. I actually prefer it, because it's quiet and private, and sometimes I want to be alone.

All right, a lot of the time I want to be alone.

I turn and leave, heading toward the bridge. Lately, it's been my favorite place. I find that I look forward to sitting in my nav chair and pulling up the star charts and just relaxing for the next few hours with an open comm channel and the stars for company.

I don't blame the others for wanting to spend time with their mates. I really don't. But once upon a time, the *Fool* felt like we were a crew of friends, making money, doing jobs, and having a good time. Now it's three couples and their fifth wheel. I don't begrudge anyone their happiness.

Being on the bridge is mine.

The doors slide open as I enter, welcoming me. Things are quiet, the screens showing alternate views of star charts with the courses I've plotted, and open space across from that. The main system scrolls through minute navigational shifts, automatically plotting and replotting with every planet, asteroid, or shipping lane we pass. My seat at the bow is empty, waiting for my return.

As I move toward it, I feel at peace. No, more than that, there's a low coil of anticipation in my belly.

Alone at last.

"Sentorr," I hear Iris call from the hallway. "Wait up."

I bite back a groan of irritation, because out of all the humans, I like Iris the most. She's sweet, thoughtful, and best of all, quieter than the other two. And because it's Iris, I wait, automatically tapping the door controls so they'll remain open.

She arrives a moment later, her radar goggles resting on top of her head and her cane in her hands. She's told me before that she doesn't mind the goggles, but they require concentration and sometimes she prefers to take them off. Her cane lightly taps against the edge of the portal into the bridge before she steps inside, and she automatically turns toward my chair. Her small human face has a bright, wide ribbon over the scars where her eyes used to be. "Are you sitting?"

"Not yet." I keep the abruptness out of my tone. "I was just about to take my station. Is something wrong?"

"No. Alyvos and I were about to go to bed anyhow." Her cheeks get a little pink, a smile on her face as she feels her way forward a step or two, her hand clasping the back of Aly's chair at his station. "I won't bother you long. I just wanted to...talk. Is everything okay? You seemed troubled tonight."

"What makes you think that?" I clasp my hands behind my back, not moving.

Iris smiles in my direction and tucks her cane under her arm. "You were quiet."

"I'm always quiet."

"This is a different kind of quiet." She tilts her head. "I was just wondering if something was bothering you."

"I'm fine." I don't know if she would understand. I'm not entirely sure I understand how I'm feeling, just that I'm impatient for her to leave so I can be alone here on the bridge. "Really. Don't worry about me."

"I was talking to Aly and we were thinking about taking a vacation when we get back from our next refuel stop. Find some planet with a nice beach and take a few days to just relax. Do you want to come? You're always welcome to hang out."

And be a third wheel instead of a fifth (or seventh) wheel? "I'm fine, truly."

"I worry you need to take a break, Sentorr. You work twice as much as anyone else." The smile she gives me is gentle, even as she runs her hands along the back of Alyvos's chair as if missing her mate's presence at her side. "I know sometimes you think we don't notice, but we do. Everyone on this ship cares about you."

She really is a good human. Alyvos is a lucky male. "I truly am fine, Iris. I enjoy working. I do." I glance down at my comm panel on the ship and see the green light that tells me I've received a ship-to-ship comm while away from my station, and my impatience grows. "I know it's hard to believe, but some of my happiest times are alone here on the bridge."

"Mmm." Iris clearly doesn't believe me. She smooths her fingers —four of them and a thumb, which still jars me—along the chair, then gives it a pat. "If you ever want to talk, you know you have a friend in me. I won't say a thing."

I glance down at the green light and do my best not to be impatient with Iris. She's trying her best to be supportive. "I do thank you, but rest assured, I'm quite fine, unlike Alyvos, who is likely ready to tear the walls down because you've been gone so long."

A brilliant smile lights up her face. "I've been gone less than five minutes."

"Precisely."

Iris chuckles and takes her cane in hand again, gliding the tip along the floor. "You have a point. All right. I just wanted to check on you." She doesn't leave, though, hesitating. "If you need someone to come and cover the shift—"

"I know," I tell her quickly. "I will knock at Alyvos's door and you will keep him company. I am aware." I pause, worried I sound abrupt. "And I do thank you, Iris. You are very kind."

She gives me another soft smile, pats Alyvos's chair, and then turns to leave. I wait until she's tapped her way off the bridge and disappeared down the hall to the living quarters before I hit the button to shut the bridge doors and then turn to my station, practically sweating with eagerness. I can't type the command to receive fast enough, my heart pounding in my chest.

It's a message from the *Little Sister,* an old junker of a Class IV freighter, run by a family of fellow pirates. It's an open message, sent on a pirate band that doesn't get much use as the common channels, but it's perfect for late-night private communications. *Did you die?* The message has no official receiver assigned, but I know it's for me. I recognize the "tone." *Fall into a wormhole? Nearest sun go supernova? What?*

I can't stop the smile that creases my face. In fact, I'm smiling so broadly that I can feel my cheeks ache. I laugh to myself at the message, then send a response. *Not dead. We celebrated a successful shipment. Took me a few to get away from the others.*

I kick my feet up on the dash, idly checking charts, system performance of the ship and nearby news feeds while waiting for the *Little Sister's* response.

It doesn't take long. *It's about keffing time. I thought I was going to be on all night by myself.*

Nope, I send back. *I'm here. Settling in for a late night?*

Yes. My brothers are asleep. Cargo is locked and loaded. Currently en route to the nearest port for some fuel, rest, relaxation, and then off we go again. The usual. You?

We just finished a delivery of worms to a trader who's taking them to the Outer Rim.

Worms, huh? Yummy. Hope those were for soil and not for eating.

Eating, I send back. *Look up inukni worms. I'll wait.*

I picture her bright blue skin and flashing white smile. Does she wear her dark hair in a braid, I wonder? Or loose? For what feels like the thousandth time since we first started our late-night chats, I try to imagine what the navigator of the *Little Sister* looks like, because I'm completely and utterly entranced with her. She's had my heart since the very first dirty joke she made across the comm bands.

I know her name is Zoey. Unusual for a mesakkah, but she says it's a family name, which isn't. I know she has three older brothers who served in the war back on Homeworld and she joined them when they started runs with the *Little Sister.* I know that they travel the same lanes we do, and that they prefer to escort personnel (aka hideaways or hostages or criminals on the run) instead of smuggling contraband like the *Fool* does. I know she loves the stars more than anything and loves to travel.

I know she's lonely and unmated, and she only spends time with her brothers and the ship. I know she's got a wickedly sharp sense of humor, and she's startling in her thinking sometimes.

In short, she's perfect for me.

I just have to convince her to leave her ship for mine. I haven't figured out how I'm going to achieve that yet, but it's my goal. Zoey will be my female if it's the last thing I do...but for now, I'm content to flirt across comm channels with her.

Wow. That is hugely gross. People do that?

They do.

You said you grew up on a farm world. Did you ever have to do that?

Once or twice when it was a bad year.

She types in something illegible that looks like a symbol.

I didn't copy your last transmission, I tell her.

Oh, sorry. That was just a sad face. Sort of. I tend to use it with my brothers a lot. It's a holdover from...well, it's just a bad habit. Nothing important. Sorry if I confused you.

Not confused. I just didn't grasp your message. I feel that way a lot lately, though.

I'm laughing, she sends. *The females again? Your ship needs a hefty dose of estrogen. It'll be good for you, Sentorr.* She knows all about my struggles to fit in with the ever-changing roles on the ship, and she thinks it's funny. I just like making her laugh, and I know she has my back, so I don't mind her amusement.

Well, one of them might be breeding, I admit, thinking of Fran and her irritable moods lately...and her fixation with mixing both sweet and sour noodles in the mess hall. *I admit it's hard to tell with humans.*

There's a really long pause, and I picture her flicking through the seven or eight monitors on her station—just like mine—looking for the best path to steer the *Little Sister* safely out of notice from nearby ships, law enforcement, and anything else that might cross their paths. I'm so fascinated by the mental image I almost miss her next transmission.

Humans?

Shocking, isn't it? It's not something I normally share with others, since they're contraband, but yes. Not just one, but three humans on board the Fool. Feel sorry for me.

I totally do, ew. You guys must be a human magnet or something.

I chuckle to myself. Sometimes I think that. I hope you don't think less of me and the crew here. I know those that co-habitate with humans are...tough to comprehend sometimes, but they really are just like you and me for the most part. Strange looking, though.

I'm just shocked you'd keep such a thing from me. I thought we were friends, Sentorr.

It's not something you bring up casually. Heading out to Saan Takhi Station, and oh, by the way, we're infested with humans.

No, I guess not. Still, wow, humans.

I'm surprised you haven't run into them much with your line of work. We're always careful not to say exactly what it is we do because it is an open ship channel, of course.

You would think, but nope. I think my brothers try to protect me from that sort of thing.

From the way she's described them, they're extremely protective, as all good mesakkah brothers are. I'm glad they're protective. *It makes me feel better knowing you're safe with them.* I hesitate, then continue on, because I'm hungry for more than just a simple conversation tonight. Maybe it's seeing how the others are with their females, and maybe I'm feeling alone. Maybe it's that she feels a little distant and I can't figure out why. *I want to hear your voice tonight, Zoey.*

Her reply is immediate. *Me too. Do we dare?*

I can wait no longer. I buzz directly over to the *Little Sister,* using a private, encoded comm band. Zoey's used to this, though—she knows exactly how I encrypt the band and picks it up right away. We've done this many times, but every time it leaves me equally tense with anticipation. "Hello again," I murmur, adjusting my earpiece so I won't miss a moment of her voice.

"Were you expecting someone else?" There's sly amusement in her voice, and just the barest hint of an accent. She speaks mesakkah nearly perfectly, but there's a lilt to certain words I haven't been able to figure out. She says she grew up in a small, insular city and hence the accent, but I don't hear that. It's familiar, and yet...not. Whatever it is, it adds a fascinating edge to everything she says.

"I'm not interested in talking to anyone else," I admit. "Where are you at?"

"Currently skirting a very busy shipping lane just outside of Andor IV. Poking at my nav charts. Watching a comet drift incredibly close to a freighter that's not paying attention and enjoying the lightshow of a distant meteor shower one system over that's just screaming for a visit. You?"

"Opening a comm line with my favorite female. You on a delivery run?" It's been days since I've talked to her and I've keffing missed the sound of her voice. It's like now that I've heard it again, I feel whole. Remade. Which is stupid, but it's true. I think about Zoey all the time—when I sleep, in the shower, when I'm around the others. I think of her when the others share affectionate caresses with their mates. I think of her when I'm alone here on deck. I think of her when I get myself a cup of noodles, because I wonder what noodles are her favorite.

I'm obsessed.

I don't care, either. If being obsessed with a female who has an attractive voice is a problem, then I am quite content to be a male with problems.

"Nah. We're wrapping up. Escorted our nice discreet couple to the nice discreet planet of their choice and are now heading discreetly back to the nearest station to refuel." She sighs. "Unfortunately, the nearest station is 3N-Station and it's kind of a pit. I swear, the air there smells like cheap meat and body odor. You ever been there?"

I can't believe it. She's so close and yet so far away. Out of all the stations I was thinking about taking the *Fool* back to for refueling, 3N was on that list. 3N is nav slang for Three Nebulas, one of the largest stations on this end of the galaxy. It's also one of the most overrun with people of every shape and size and species, and she's not wrong about the smell. I was going to skip it...but now that I know she's heading in that direction? I lean over my monitor and tap out a few coordinate changes. We'll spend a bit more fuel, but I'll tell Kivian to take it out of my share if we need to. "I've been to 3N many, many times. Aren't they having trouble with pirates lately?" Iris has been telling me about that. She likes to listen in on scattered comm bands in the hopes of hearing information we can use.

"Pirates, huh? You don't say." Her tone is sly, teasing.

"Yep. Pirates." We both appreciate the joke for a moment, and then I press on. "What would you say if I told you we're heading that way, too? We just happened to offload our shipment and we're heading in that direction."

"Huh. Isn't it a little out of the way from where you were running? I thought you were taking goods out to Primus's third moon?" I can hear the confusion in her voice and the light tap of her fingers on her monitors. For some reason, she types very loudly and quickly. It's odd but adorable.

Can't pull one over on a navigator. I'm both amused and chagrined that she's seen through me so quickly. "It's a little bit of a fuel-burner, but we have a contact to meet there." I manually change a few more settings, adjusting the ship's course as I do. Given time, the *Fool* will chart her own course as long as there's an end point, but I like giving my hands something to do.

Zoey's silence makes me nervous.

We've been talking on bands for months. Longer than that.

Maybe a year now. Every night, we send messages to each other, and over the last few months, we've been doing private comms. Intimate comms. I thought we were close, but her silence is a bad sign.

Maybe she's shy and waiting for me to say more. It's already out in the open, so I plunge ahead. I pull up the location of the *Little Sister* on my charts, since I know their particular signal. "It looks like you should be there tomorrow, if my charts are right. We'll be there the day after." I pause, then continue. "I want to meet you, Zoey."

I want that more than anything. You're my mate. I'm tired of just wishing for you. I want to hold you.

She makes a soft sound in her throat. "I'd love to meet you, too, Sentorr."

Her voice is breathless and sweet, and my body tenses with need. Hearing her husky, soft voice makes my sac tighten, and I know my cock's hard. She arouses me like nothing I've ever keffing seen and I haven't even looked her in the eye. I don't need to. I know she's perfect.

Which is why her next words feel like a punch in the gut. "—But we're just doing a quick stopover. We're not staying for long. There's another passenger we have to shuttle and he's making noises about extra jingle in our pockets if we get there faster, so you know my brothers are all over that." Zoey hesitates. "I'm sorry. Maybe next time?"

I grunt. "Maybe so." I punch the coordinates to 3N anyhow, though I feel like shoving the entire monitor off my station and kicking it once or twice.

"Don't be sad," she tells me, and her voice is light and coy, a frisky note edging in. "I'll just have to make it up to you."

A groan tears from my throat, and I glance over at the bridge doors—closed—before rubbing my hand against the front of my trou. "You're in one of those moods tonight, I see."

"God, I'm 'in one of those moods' every time we talk. I'm like that every time I hear your voice." And she lets out this keffing sexy little whimper that tells me she's touching herself.

It's too much. The throb of my cock becomes aching, and I quickly unfasten my clothes, freeing it. "Let me see your face tonight," I demand. "Call me with a visual comm, not this audio shit."

"I can't," Zoey whispers. "I don't like my face...I'm too ugly. I don't want you to see it."

We've had this conversation a dozen times, easily. She refuses to go to visual communication and says it's because of her face. I don't care if she has a nose bigger than her horns, I want to see her face. I know I'll find her lovely. I hate nothing about her, and not seeing her face feels more like torture than anything. "Zoey, you know I don't care—"

"I care," she says stubbornly. "You're killing my lady boner with this, Sentorr. If you want to talk to me, it has to be like this. Please."

There's a quiet note of desperation in her "please" that makes me sigh. I don't understand her fear—she's so brave over the comm, and from what she's told me about her brothers, she's equally bold with them. "You frustrate me."

"But you love me," she teases back, the playful note back in her voice, along with an edge of hope.

Funny how she throws "love" around. That's a human term if there ever was one. Maybe she picked it up on one of her runs. I grin to myself, thinking how apt the term is. "I do love you. You have my heart. You know this."

"Well if I do, then can we not argue with each other? I'd much rather engage in some dirty talk. I could...tell you what my hand's on right now."

"Your cunt?" I murmur the words low, because even though I'm alone on the bridge, it needs to be a private thing between us. I want to share my mate with no one.

Zoey gives a trilling little sigh. "It is so filthy when you say that. God, it makes me wet."

I stroke a hand over my cock. "You'd better be touching yourself," I growl.

"Oh, I am. Are you stroking your big thick cock?" Her voice is throaty. "I'm imagining you touching it, the head slick with pre-cum."

The breath hitches in my throat, because she's not wrong. I'm so hard for her that I ache, and my pulse throbs through my body with the need for release. "I am."

"You should picture me with my mouth on you," she says. "Licking you up and down like I've never tasted anything better."

As always, I'm shocked by her words—shocked AND aroused. "Plas-film?" I murmur thickly.

"Never."

I shudder, nearly coming at that. Zoey has such a dirty mouth. She knows just what to say to make me come quickly and hard. "You...you'd put your mouth directly on me?"

"All over your cock," she agrees. "I'd rub it all over my face, hungry for more. I bet you're so big that it'd stretch my lips just trying to fit you into my mouth."

A hard grunt escapes my throat and I stroke my cock, hard. I'm already ready to come, my sac tight with need. "I want to hear you come first, Zoey. Those are the rules."

"Mmm," she says, and then I hear her moan lightly. My ears prick as I can barely make out the sound of her rubbing her wet flesh, and I imagine her fingers gliding between her folds. It's enough to make a man insane with lust, but I manage to hold out, slowly stroking my cock and murmuring encouragement as she works her cunt until she gives a soft, muffled cry that pierces my soul. With a groan, I give my cock another few rough strokes until I come, too.

Zoey sighs happily. "I always feel so naughty after we do that."

"Next time, I want to do it looking into your face," I tell her. "I mean it when I say I want to meet you. I don't care what you look like. I just want to hold your hand and touch your face."

"Maybe we'll both be in the same place at the same time," she says wistfully. "At some point."

"Maybe." I'm going to make it happen sooner rather than later. As the conversation turns towards idle chatter, I keep messing with the *Fool's* current course. If I keep making minute changes, I can shave time off of our travel. A minute here, ten minutes there. If I keep doing that for the next eighteen hours or so, we should make it to 3N late, late tomorrow.

And hopefully the *Little Sister* will still be there.

Because I want to claim my female. I'm tired of waiting for maybe, or for someday.

2

ZOEY

*a*fter I hang up with Sentorr, it's nearly time for Adiron to wake up and relieve me of the night shift. It'll give me a chance to catch a nap before my three brothers descend on 3N and wreak havoc. I haven't yet decided if I'll go—on the one hand, I've been cooped up in the *Sister* for a long damn time, but on the other, visiting stations isn't all that fun. Every look I get makes me wary and anxious. Adiron can have fun no matter the place, but I know it bugs Mathiras and Kaspar when I'm miserable and they bail out early because I'm unhappy.

Which just makes me even more miserable, because they deserve shore leave as much as the next person.

I give my station one last caress, picturing Sentorr's face before I get up to run to the lavatory. I need to wash up before Adiron wakes and smells the scent of arousal on the air. I learned the hard way that their noses are way more sensitive than mine, and the incident when I was fourteen and had to explain to my three older brothers that I was masturbating? That's a moment I'd like to never live again.

So I rush to the lavatory and turn on the water, then pause. I'm still thinking of Sentorr's face. His ship doesn't have an ID tag on it, but I looked him up on old prison records. The only holo I have of him is an old 2-D, but it's burned into my mind (and might be printed out and tucked under my pillow). He's got tall, arching horns, a too-serious face, and the most impressively plush mouth that should have never been on a male and yet somehow looks perfect and sexy on him.

My hand slides back to my pussy, and I start to touch myself again. God, I have it bad. I give myself a quick rub to release, and then plunge my hands under the spray of water. For the first time, I look up in the mirror at my face.

Humans?

Shocking, isn't it?

Feel sorry for me.

Feel sorry for me. Those four words are burned into my brain as I stare at my human nose, human eyes, human mouth, and horn-less head. I hate my face. I hate the freckles on my nose, the mousey brown hair, the skin that's not quite white, not quite pink, not quite gold but some pasty shade in between. I don't have the gorgeous blue mesakkah skin. I don't have horns or the plated brow that looks so ruggedly fierce. I'm all soft and wimpy with no plating anywhere and boobs that stick out no matter how much I bind them down.

Feel sorry for me.

Kef me, I didn't expect it to hurt so much. I know most mesakkah have a very unpleasant view of humans. We're somewhere between a taboo fucktoy and a trained dog. In the ten years since

I was snatched by slavers, the only other humans I've seen are other women who have been forced into slavery, black market playthings that are doomed to have a shitty life under an alien master's thumb.

I touch my face, wondering if I'm pretty to other humans. My brothers say I look fine—well, Adiron says I'm ugly enough to peel paint off the hull of a freighter, but Adiron's a keffing idiot. I wonder if...if Sentorr wasn't disgusted by humans, would he find me attractive? Or am I too freakish for him? The few mesakkah that I've met that have seen my real face (other than my brothers) looked at me pityingly.

I think if Sentorr looked at me with pity or disgust, I'd die. My heart hurts at the thought. I know it bothers him that I won't let him see my face, but...I can't. I know our flirtation is forbidden, but I can't let it go. It's the only thing I have that's truly mine, and I don't want to give it up.

I can never meet him, of course, but I can always dream about it. It's nice to have something—or someone—to look forward to, someone that makes me breathless and full of happiness at the sound of their voice. Our late-night flirtations started out as just that—a fun, silly way to pass the time. It was months before we got past jokes and shared griping about the latest meteor shower or a law enforcement vehicle waiting to snipe people out near the rings of Cassa IV. He was just a buddy.

It's only recently that it's become...problematic.

Because he wants more. And I want more. I scrub my face, my hands, and then between my legs. It can't be more. It can't.

Feel sorry for me.

BANG BANG BANG BANG.

"Did you keffing die in there?"

"Kef off," I shout back to Adiron. "Can't I get five keffing minutes to myself when I'm on the john?"

"It's been longer than that," my brother calls back. "What the kef did you eat?"

I growl and finish washing my hands, dry them, and then slam the door open to look at Adiron's goofy grin. "I hate you."

"No, Runt, you love me." He grabs me around the neck, tucking me under one of those enormous blue arms and noogies the hell out of my head. "You looooooove me."

"Haaaaate," I snarl back, squirming out of his grasp. "You're such a creep."

"You're stinking up the lavatory and I need to be able to breathe while I'm on the bridge," he tells me, moving to my station and plopping his big feet up on the counter like he owns it.

I make an indignant sound and go slap his enormous boot. "Go sit at your own station!"

"Can't," he tells me, crossing his arms and giving me a toothy, fanged smile. "It's a mess. You wanna clean it for me?"

I know he's just getting under my skin, but it works every keffing time and I mime strangling him. "It's your damn mess. You go clean it!"

"Nah." He takes his feet down when I smack them again and swivels in my chair. "Did you change our course?"

I can feel my face get hot with a flush. "What? No. Why would I do that?"

"You tell me, Runt." He pokes a few buttons. "Looks like you're changing our arrival time at 3N. There a reason for a delay?"

"Is there a delay? I didn't realize." I cross my arms now, feigning ignorance. "You can change it. I don't care what time we get there."

He narrows his eyes at me, then sweeps his long black braid back over his shoulder and begins to reroute our course. "You sure you're okay? It's not like you to plot a garbage run like this. That's more Kaspar's thing."

I drum my fingers against my arm because...he's not wrong. Kaspar's as reckless as he is brave, and that's why he's not in charge of navigation anymore. That's why it's my baby. I was hoping to maybe delay the *Sister* by a few hours...just in case...

But that's stupid. More than that, I KNOW it's stupid. And yet I can't help but wonder... I shift anxiously on my feet. "Hey, Adiron, can I ask you a question?"

"No, I didn't eat those Earth tarts you like so much," he mutters under his breath as he taps into my panel, remapping my course to the more efficient one it was earlier.

"Pop Tarts," I correct. Even though I haven't been on Earth since I was ten, I still miss the junk foods I had as a kid.

"Might as well eat a tube of cryo preservative," he tells me. "Probably as healthy."

I make a face at the back of his head. "Do you think I'm pretty? For a human?"

He swivels in my chair, his expression completely aghast. "Did... did you just ask me if I find you pretty? Your brother?" He presses a hand to his mouth and acts like he's going to vomit. "I think I'm going to lose my lunch."

I smack his shoulder and storm off. "Forget I asked."

"I'm gonna kack up my breakfast all over your monitors if you ask me that sort of thing again," he calls after my back. "Night night!"

I head to my room, frustrated, and punch my pillow a few times imagining that it's Adiron's dopey face. Of all my brothers, I'm probably closest to him, but he's also the most irritating, unserious person I've ever met.

I should have asked Mathiras. He would have given me a straight answer, at least.

I punch my pillow again, but I'm more frustrated at the situation than at Adiron. I love my brothers. I do. I love them with every fiber of my being. Despite the fact that they're a trio of space pirates, they're the best men I've ever met. I'm eternally grateful that they've been so very good to me.

When I was ten, I was stolen from my bed in the middle of the night and woke up in a rundown space freighter with a bunch of adult women. Back then, I didn't know what was going on. Adult me now knows that I was kidnapped to be a pet—or sex slave—to be sold on the black market. The race that captured me—the szzt —work with a lot of other alien races to bring them slaves. Lucky for me, my three mesakkah brothers saw easy pickings and took over the ship. They dumped the humans off to the nearest trader and turned a profit, but they weren't interested in a child human (aka me) and so my brothers kept me for a while longer.

I think they thought I was cute, like a stray puppy.

After letting me run wild on their ship for a while, I vaguely remember sitting at Kaspar's nav station while he was on duty and distracted, and thinking that the maps that glided over the screen showing an endless sea of stars reminded me of video games from home. I started tapping things, trying to "win" the level, and when I didn't, I cussed a blue streak in mesakkah. I shocked all three brothers, who hadn't realized that I was listening to everything they said.

I had my mouth washed out with soap...and they kept me.

Over the years, we've become closer than family. Adiron, Kaspar and Mathiras have family back on Homeworld. The va Sithai name is an old, honorable one. But they don't go home much, and I get the impression their folks aren't happy with them, so they're content to stay out in space and run wild.

And I run wild with them. We're a great team. For the last ten years, the *Little Sister* (named after me) has been my home. The three brothers taught me how to speak mesakkah so I wouldn't have to rely on a translator, educated me in things I would actually need to know out in space, and have basically treated me like an equal despite my human status. I can change every filter in the *Sister's* engine, plot out a course across the galaxy, and shoot a blaster with accuracy. I can cuss in thirteen languages, play a mean game of Sticks, and eat more noodles than Adiron. I've taken over the navigation duties from Kaspar, who's happier being in charge of security and odd jobs than cooped up at the nav station all day long.

Here, I fit in. It doesn't matter that I'm a girl, or a human. My three big brothers have always made me feel welcome. Like I'm part of the team.

I know how rare and special that is, and I'm grateful. It's why I'll never leave them. They love me and I love them.

I'm lucky. I'm really lucky. Humans are considered contraband in every corner of the galaxy except the Sol solar system, where humankind lives blissfully unaware that space is teeming with aliens that dislike them (or only like them as slaves). I have to avoid notice by anyone that might drag me to the authorities, because humans confiscated by the law are never seen again.

At least other aliens only try to steal me as a sex toy.

My protective brothers are very aware that my humanity's a problem. It's why they were so insistent I learn mesakkah and nagged me about my pronunciation until I was able to speak fluently without much of an accent. My brothers don't even allow me to go without a disguise on the seediest of stations. It doesn't matter that the law won't be around—they don't want anyone else stealing me either. Every time I leave the ship, I have to be accompanied by one of them to protect me, and I'm armed to the teeth. I'm also dressed in heavy robes to hide my breasts and lack of tail, extremely tall shoes, and false horns. My face is disguised by a holo that works fine as long as no one touches me or gets too close. The holo makes me nervous, though, so most of the time I just stay on the ship.

And...even with the company of my brothers, it does get lonely. It shouldn't matter that sometimes the ship gets awfully quiet when I'm on an overnight by myself, or when they all head out to the nearest space station to spend some quality time in a cantina with space hoes. I try not to let it bother me that I don't have any female friends, or that I haven't kissed anyone. That the closest I'll ever get to romance is my stupid hand and a couple of sleazy porn vids I stole from Adiron's file dump.

Maybe that's why Sentorr's friendship is so precious to me. When I talk to him, I feel like a normal woman. Like I'm not a freak. With him, I'm sexy, bold, and confident. I'm bold around my brothers, of course, but...it's different.

I can't lose Sentorr or his friendship...which is why we can never, ever meet.

I INHALE DEEPLY, standing close to Mathiras so I don't trip over my enormous stilt-like shoes. "Ahh, smell that? I'd recognize that Three Nebulas funk anywhere."

My brother snorts and puts a hand on my shoulder. "Stay close. Hood on."

I just roll my eyes, because we've been to a hundred stations and the drill never changes. Robes on and high at the neck. Gloves over hands. No human skin showing. Holo on over my face, hood clasped over my fake horns to hide the fact that they're strapped to my head.

Oh, and when we're in public? I respond to the name Vanora. It's apparently the name of their sister back home that I've never met, who has three children and a mate and hates the thought of piracy. She'd never be out in the far reaches of space, slumming it on the docks of 3N with ooli and szzt and mesakkah everywhere. I watch with interest as a trandarian (aka lizard man) storms past in a swirl of cape, a contingent of armed a'ani clones at his side. "Someone's got important business," I murmur, my pirate's eye sizing him up.

"I'm liking what I see," Kaspar adds.

"Too many a'ani," Mathiras says in a clipped tone. "If he's got one troop with him, he'll have more."

Sure enough, the moment the words come out of my brother's mouth, another cluster of clones heads down the hall after the first, their bright red skin obvious even in the dirty lighting of the station.

"Kef it, I hate it when Mathiras is right," Adiron grumbles.

"Let's just get to our dock and meet our contacts," Mathiras says, all business. "This is my least favorite station."

"Ugliest hookers, too," Adiron adds, and Kaspar snickers.

"Gross," I chime in. "Stay classy, Adi."

"Don't make me noogie you," he says, tail flicking.

I regret the day I ever noogied him and showed him what it was. I make a face at him as the clones pass by, not even glancing in our direction.

"All of you, stop bickering," Mathiras says, pulling out his datapad. A ship nearby has just let out her passengers, and the low-ceilinged hall is currently flooding with all kinds of people of every shape and size, and we're forced to press against the wall to let them pass. Kaspar watches them with interest, but Mathiras ignores them, tapping away on his datapad. "Now that we've refueled, I'd prefer to conduct business quickly and get the kef out of here."

"No cantina?" Adiron asks, disappointment in his voice.

"No cantina," Mathiras agrees.

"You said they were ugly anyhow," Kaspar teases, his eye on the a'ani in the distance. No doubt he's trying to think of a way to overtake them and snatch the purse of their fat client. Kaspar likes terrible odds. He's as dumb as Adiron in his own way.

"You can still put your dick in ugly," I say, gesturing. "You just turn 'em around and—" I go quiet at Mathiras's glare and give him a meek look. "Just trying to be helpful."

Adiron chuckles.

"All of you, simmer down." He taps the datapad again. "We've got two scores today if we play our cards right. Two deliveries. One's a passenger pickup at dock Twenty-Seven-B and the other's cargo at dock Two-Zed. I figure we can split up and take care of things."

"I'll take passengers," Kaspar says. Of course he would. He loves the excitement, since most of our passengers are the squirrelly sort.

"I'll go with...are they hot passengers?" Adiron asks, and we all ignore him.

"Good. I'll take Vanora with me since she's along." Mathiras doesn't need to say more. I never get to go on the more dangerous missions, and sometimes you have to bust the passengers out the hard way. I can't run for shit in these shoes, so it makes sense, but it's still disappointing.

I cross my arms. "Cargo it is. What kind of cargo?"

"Something about a shipment of Class II weaponry. I didn't get details from the *Fool*." He's already tucking his datapad away. "Come on."

I feel an icy haze wash move over me, like a wave of needles prickling down my spine. "The...what?" I'm suddenly having trouble breathing.

"What's the what?" Mathiras turns back to me, frowning.

"You deaf, dummy?" Adiron asks, reaching over to stick a big finger in my very human ear under my hood.

I swat his big hand away. "The ship," I manage to choke out. "What's the cargo ship?"

"It's the something or other Fool. Another corsair group, I think. They're offloading cargo. Didn't want the job anymore or some such."

I think I'm going to be sick.

This...is a problem.

My brothers don't know about my flirtation with Sentorr. If they did, they'd freak out. They'd worry that I'm being unsafe, or that he's taking advantage of me. Any chance I have to talk to him would be shut down immediately and I'd never get a moment of privacy on the bridge again.

I'd never get to hear Sentorr's voice again. I'm not ready to give that up yet.

I need to do something. I can't meet him. I can't have my brothers meet him because if they do, Sentorr's bound to comment about me. I have to keep the two worlds separate for a little while longer.

So I grab Mathiras's arm. "We can't. If it's the *Lovesick Fool,* we can't meet them. Please."

My brother narrows his eyes at me. He's silent for a long, tense moment that makes me want to squirm.

"What's wrong with the *Fool*? You piss 'em off?" Adiron wants to know. Kaspar just frowns in my direction.

They're all staring at me and I know they're going to want answers. Real answers.

"Zo—Vanora," Mathiras says, and his tone is warning. I know he's frustrated because he's normally the only one that remembers my fake name. That little slip is very telling. "What did you do?"

I grimace, trying to determine how much to confess. As people continue to mill about the crowded docks, my anxiety heightens. I catch a glimpse of blue mesakkah skin in the distance and see a big ugly male with a smiling human female collared and chained at his side. Kef me. That can't be a coincidence. Sentorr said his crewmates had human mates, so that has to be one of them.

"Well?" Mathiras prompts.

I clench my gloved hands, then decide to spill. "I might have a flirtation thing going on with their navigator."

Kaspar groans as if pained.

"What?" I ask defensively. I reach out and smack his shoulder. "It's just late-night talk. That's all."

"If that's all it is, you wouldn't ask us not to meet them," Kaspar returns, and gives my shoulder a light tap in response, the gentle brotherly version of a teasing shove. "Does he know..."

"My secret?" I prompt.

"Yeah, that you still wet the bed?" Adiron adds, then flings his arm around my neck, tugging on my hood. For a moment, I think he's going to noogie me again—and then he pauses, as if it just occurred to him that he can't.

"Har de har," I say, elbowing Adiron in the side. "And no, he doesn't know anything about me. Just that I'm a nav and your little sister." I emphasize the last part, letting them know that I'm not stupid enough to reveal the truth.

"But he does know you," Mathiras continues. When I nod, he exchanges a look back to my other brothers. "All right. I'll take Vanora back to the *Sister*. You two go and retrieve our passengers, and let's just get out of here. I'll send a comm to the *Fool* and let them know something came up and we won't be retrieving the shipment."

Hot, girly tears of relief flood my eyes and I sniffle, emotional. "Thanks, guys. I'm sorry I keffed everything up."

"You didn't kef anything up," Kaspar says, ever my defender. "It's no big deal."

Adiron just hugs me and Mathiras pats my shoulder.

"We're a team. All of us," Mathiras says. "If this is a job you want us to avoid, we avoid it. Simple as that."

I nod, feeling lucky to have them as my brothers.

"Let's not waste any time, then," Mathiras says, putting his datapad back into its holster in his belt. "The sooner we get off this station, the better."

Just like that, it's decided. There won't be a meeting with the *Fool*. There won't be smack talk (at least not yet) about me killing a job before it ever starts. No one's going to give me grief about my flirtation. I'm part of the team and because I said no, it's handled. The miserable knot in my stomach starts to unwind. Kaspar and Adiron take off, the latter giving me a squeeze before jogging after Kaspar.

It's just me and Mathiras. He gives me a long look, then gestures back down the way we came. "Let's go back, shall we?"

"Yep," I tell him, a little too eagerly.

I turn and take his arm, just like the mesakkah lady I'm supposed to be. We step back onto the automated walkway and start zipping down one of the many cramped tunnels of the station, leaving the starboard-side docks behind—and the *Fool*.

As we glide past, I catch a flash of blue skin and horns on the opposite walkway and automatically turn. The breath catches in my lungs as I recognize the hard, solemn face and that pouty mouth.

It's Sentorr, and he's more gorgeous than I ever thought he'd be. There's something about his physical presence that's harder that I imagined, and more virile. His hair's shorter than it was in the photo, cropped to regulation length as if he's about to head off into service with Homeworld troops. And his horns...god.

They could give a girl fantasies, those horns.

I sigh dreamily, craning my neck as he whizzes past. He doesn't notice me watching him, his head bent over his datapad. He's beautiful...and he can never be mine.

I'm surprised at how much it hurts to realize that.

SENTORR

I wait by the *Fool's* cargo bay doors, sitting atop the crate of plas-rifles and stare down at the notification on my datapad.

Change of plans. Can't take job. - LS

That's it. That's the only notification I get. The *Little Sister* isn't coming. Zoey isn't coming.

They were here on the station, and I missed them.

I don't know if I feel disgusted or disappointed. Zoey knew I was going to be here. Hell, I threw up that cargo suggestion just to make sure that her ship'd be here at the same time mine was. When Mathiras va Sithai accepted the rendezvous, I felt elation because I knew that Zoey would be on the station. It'd be inevitable that we'd meet. I don't even mind losing out on a crate of expensive rifles—my share of a botched job a few runs back—just because it means I get to see her.

For her crew to cancel on me at the last moment tells me one thing and one thing alone: Zoey doesn't want to meet me. She either got scared and backed out, or had no plans to meet me at all, ever.

Hopelessly, I gaze around the busy cargo bay of 3N. Maybe I'm wrong. Maybe I'll wait a few more minutes and a pretty female mesakkah with a smoky voice will make her way around a nearby ship and it'll be her after all. That it was a big misunderstanding and she'd never leave the station without saying hello to me first.

That she wants more from our clandestine friendship than just a few dirty words.

But no one ever comes.

It seems all of the feelings I have for Zoey are one-sided. If she cared anything at all for me, she'd have been here.

The realization's like a knife in the gut.

3

ZOEY

I wait almost a full day before I decide to send a comm request to Sentorr. It's not a good sign that he hasn't even sent me an offline message. Normally my private chat logs are full of notes from him over the course of the day, and I feel the lack of them acutely.

He's avoiding me deliberately.

It's my own fault. I pulled a jerk move, bailing out. How rare is it that we happened to be at the same station at the same time? He must have burned a ton of fuel just to be at Three Nebulas Station at the same time I was there, and I was the dick that was too cowardly to show up. I feel rotten about it, but I know it was the right thing to do.

Sentorr wouldn't understand that I'm human. He'd be disgusted. Betrayed. I'd lose him either way. At least this way, his mental image of me is still a pleasant one. In his eyes, I'm just a mesakkah woman playing hard to get. I'm not a gross human.

Feel sorry for me.

I don't want to feel sorry for him. I want him to love me even if I can't have him. Irritated, I swipe at my eyes before opening a comm link at my station. It's late at night and I'm alone on the bridge, as usual. My brothers, thank the stars, didn't give me shit when we got back to the *Sister*. Maybe they realized I was feeling fragile and left me alone. Bad enough that I cost us money and disappointed them.

Sentorr doesn't pick up my connection request.

Pissy and frustrated, I send it through again. And again. I know he's on the bridge. He's like me—he practically lives there. After five tries with no response, I give up on the connection request and change it to an audio request—the interplanetary dashboard version of a phone call.

Immediately, he picks up.

"Sentorr?" I ask, even though I know it's him.

"Feel like talking now?" His tone is bitter. "I'm rather busy, Zoey."

"We had to bail out early," I tell him lamely. "Work came up. You know how it is."

"I see."

"Please don't be mad at me," I whisper into the comm receiver. "I need you to be my friend."

My computer panel buzzes. It's a visual communication request from the *Fool*. Kef me. "Accept," Sentorr says flatly. "If you want to talk to me, that's how I want to do it."

"I can't," I tell him, panicked. I could go get my holo and flip it on, but they look grainy and unnatural in visual comms. The holo's meant to be a visual distortion and it doesn't carry through over the airwaves. He'll know I'm a phony immediately. "I can't, Sentorr. Please."

"Because you're ugly?" The hardness in his tone softens. "You let me be the judge of that. Send me a direct feed and we can talk face to face. I don't care what you look like. I never have."

He would if he knew I was human. At least then we'd be the same species. I wouldn't be disgusting in his eyes, barely sentient. "I..." I want to tell him that it's what I want, more than anything. But my throat locks up. "I can't."

Sentorr makes a frustrated sound. "I love you, Zoey. Don't be like this. Show me who you are. I won't care."

"Love?" Hearing the word startles me. It's not a mesakkah expression. "First time I've heard that word come from blue lips."

"It's a human expression."

"Guess they're not all bad, huh?" I can't resist twisting the knife, just a little.

"Not all bad, no." He sounds thoughtful, not revolted.

I waver. I should show him my face. Get this over with. Show him why I can't be the woman he wants me to be. It'd end things between us, but in a way, it'd be a blessing, wouldn't it? I wouldn't be stringing him along any more. He'd be free to move on to someone else...except I don't want him to keffing move on to someone else. Still, he deserves the truth. My hand hovers near the visual feed button on my control panels.

A red light pings off to one side. Distress beacon. Asteroid.

"I have to go," I tell him quickly, taking the coward's way out. "There's an incoming distress call from a nearby asteroid. I'll call you back, all right?"

"Do what you must, Zoey," Sentorr says abruptly, and then hangs up.

I stare at my terminals in shock, ice in my veins. That was so sudden. Does that mean he's abandoning me and our friendship?

A split second later, my personal comm channel shows up with a message. Even as the distress signal pings again, I click on my private comm.

I'll be here waiting. —S

Warmth floods through me again, and I smile even as I answer the distress call and send an alert to wake up my sleeping brothers.

SENTORR

I'm thoughtful as I stare at my monitors. There's star charts and fuel logs on every screen, but I don't see them. I'm lost in thought, my focus on the female half a galaxy away who's answering a random distress call—probably so they can rob whatever ship is stranded nearby—and yet won't send me a single visual communication.

It's strange how Zoey can be so bold about some things and so very shy and frightened of others. She speaks more plainly than any mesakkah woman I've ever met. She's unafraid and even downright crude in some of her mating talk, and half the time she instigates our sexy late-night conversations, which tells me she wants them just as much as I do.

But she won't show me her face.

The bridge's doors chime. "Iris on bridge," the computer calls out a split second before the human woman pads forward. She's wearing one of Alyvos's tunics wrapped around her body, his loose pants flapping on her slender legs. Her normal blindfold is gone and the scars over her eyesockets are glaringly bold against her pale face. "Can't sleep," she tells me, even as she yawns and moves unerringly toward Alyvos's station. "Bad dreams."

"It's Alyvos's job to make sure you don't have them," I say absently as I turn back toward my monitors. "But you're welcome to keep me company."

She chuckles lightly and I hear her sit down. "He needs his sleep. I've kept him up for the last three nights. I thought I'd have pity on him tonight and just stay awake until I pass out from sheer exhaustion. What's the news?"

"No news," I tell her, crossing my arms and glancing over at my screens. "All's quiet."

"That's boring," Iris says in her gentle voice. "How are you doing? You seem unsettled today."

I glance over at her, turning my chair to face in her direction. She has her hand on her chin and her face is tilted toward me, intently listening to my body language. "Do I?"

"Yes. Your movements are harder than they normally are. Jerkier. You seem tense."

Funny how Iris is the most perceptive one on the ship and she's blind. No one else has realized what I've been struggling with, and for the first time, I spit it out. I need to talk to someone about Zoey, because she's got me utterly turned inside out. "I...I've met someone."

"I knew it!" She sits up, her smile growing wider. "I told Alyvos there was a reason you were on the bridge all the time. You talk to her here? It's a long-distance thing, yes?"

Long-distance? It's an unusual term to describe what we have, but apt. "I suppose you could call it that. She's on another corsair ship."

"Ah. Is that why we rushed to 3N? Alyvos was wondering about that." Her expression is bright with interest. "I won't say a thing if you don't want me to, but I was curious. I thought it might have something to do with a woman, given that you were hiding up here all the time."

"Not hiding," I bluster. It's not that I don't like spending time with the crew. I just value my quiet more than the rest of them. "I enjoy being up here. I love this ship. It's not all due to her."

"I love this ship, too," Iris says. "But I've heard that everyone finds it crowded lately."

"Mm." I keep my answer vague, because I don't want to hurt her feelings. The truth is that when Fran arrived, it felt like an extra. Then Cat arrived, and things felt a little tighter, but Cat was small and always cleaning up after Tarekh, so it wasn't egregious. But when Iris arrived, it felt as if the ship hit capacity. More than capacity. We're always tripping over each other and it's rare that you can enter a room and not encounter at least one other person. The *Fool's* a great ship but she's not built to hold seven people on a regular basis. It's one reason why I'm on the bridge so much—nights here are the only quiet place on the ship.

I don't want Iris to feel as if she's a burden, though. Fran would ignore any such suggestion. Cat would fight you over it. But Iris? She's so sensitive and sweet that she would take it to heart, and everyone on the ship's protective of her. "It's just taking a little getting used to," I finally say. "I'm sure we'll manage." For all that I'm not a fan of having that many humans on board, I don't want them to go, either. Iris is a good companion and she makes my friend so happy. Cat's amusing and she loves Tarekh fiercely...and she's small enough to fit into the narrowest of pipes and clean the *Fool* from the inside out. And Fran? She's practically an extension of Kivian himself... except sometimes I think she's got more of a business mind than he does. Our captain's easily distracted by fashionable clothing.

No, even though I've dragged my feet over each and every addition to the crew, they're family. I know what it's like to be lonely, and when I see the happiness in each of my friends, I don't begrudge them their mates.

It just makes me want Zoey more. Zoey, who won't even send me a video communication of herself.

Iris straightens. "Oh. I'm not interrupting you and your girlfriend right now, am I? By being here? I didn't think about it."

I shake my head, then remember she can't see and feel like a fool. "It's fine. She had to go anyhow. Distress signal."

"There's a lot of those lately. When you talk to her again, tell her to avoid the asteroids." She tucks Alyvos's tunic tighter around her body and leans back in his chair, picking up his earpiece.

"Wait," I call out before she can put the earpiece in. "What's this about asteroids?"

She tilts her head, the scars on her face obscene and blatant against her skin. "You haven't heard? Didn't you get the message I sent to everyone's inbox?"

The humans have odd terms for personal communications. I know what she's referring to, and I'm ashamed to admit that I've been letting mine pile up over the last few days. I've been so frustrated and turned around with Zoey and my race to 3N to meet up with her that I've ignored everything else. "What's going on with asteroids?"

"There's a group of szzt pirates on the prowl. They're staking out asteroids and sending out distress calls, and when the ship arrives to help them out, they disable communications with a jammer, then murder the crew and strip down their ship for parts. It's happened at least twice lately at other stations. It's all over the news out at Guarda XIV."

Guarda XIV? That's a water-moon colony in this system...and remarkably close to 3N. I feel a cold chill go down my spine, my tail twitching at the thought. Didn't Zoey say they were getting a distress call from the nearest asteroid? Of course, they're a corsairing ship themselves, so they should be fine. No doubt they'd turn the tables on any pirate waiting for them and end up robbing THEM.

Still. I grunt at Iris to let her know I heard her, then turn to my monitors. It's only been a few minutes since I heard from Zoey. If they're answering a true, legit distress call, she'll be busy for a while. Even so, I type out a quick message to her. *Be careful out there. Word is that there's pirates sending out bogus distress signals in this system. Watch your backs.*

I watch my panels for a moment, waiting, holding my breath.

A moment later, the response I'm dreading arrives. **SIGNAL JAMMED**, the screen reads. **NO CONNECTION TO RECEIVING SHIP.**

Kef.

Kef me. I type furiously, slamming my hand over the nearest star chart to bring it active. "Iris, wake the others and tell them that the *Little Sister's* in trouble. I'm turning us around." I pull up the last known signal of the *Little Sister,* tracking from Zoey's last message to me.

When I see Guarda XIV pop up on the screen, my gut feels like a block of ice.

"I'll get the others," Iris says, and leaves me to my station.

4

ZOEY

"*We* are definitely up a kef creek without a keffing paddle," Kaspar says from his hiding place across from me, his blaster cocked and ready to fire.

I don't correct him on his bastardization of that particular Earth saying. I mean, he's not wrong. We are totally fucked at the moment. I knew piracy was a dangerous profession, of course, but I never thought I'd end my days on a gods-forsaken chunk of asteroid to some szzt bastards who want to pirate OUR pirate ship.

"I should have known better about the distress signal. Oldest trick in the keffing book," I tell my brothers.

"Don't blame yourself," Mathiras says. He's at my side and constantly keeps trying to tuck me behind him so he can block their shots with his body. Of course, I don't want him to die for my sake, so I keep sneaking under his arm and returning fire. "We all thought this might be easy prey."

"We need a distraction," I tell them. We're pinned behind a cluster of rocky formations on the asteroid's surface, and the only thing keeping us anchored to the rock itself are our grav boots. I'm breathing so hard that my helmet's fogging with my nervous panting, though. My brothers are totally calm, unlike me.

Kaspar even seems to be enjoying himself. He looks over at us and gives a wild grin. "We could try throwing Adiron at them. When they're knocked down by his overfed body we can make a break to get back to the ship."

At his side, Adiron shoves Kaspar good-naturedly. "Or we just wait because we know your impatient ass is going to race out there and get into a fistfight." Kaspar just shoves him back.

"We're not throwing anyone and we're not getting into fistfights, you two idiots," Mathiras says in a tired voice. "Let's just get back to the *Sister* and we can figure out our plans there. Zo, how are you on oxygen?"

Shit, I guess he hears my panicked breathing. Well, that and humans respire slightly faster than mesakkah. I keep forgetting that part. I check my breather's filters and I'm a little distressed at the readings. "I've got ten minutes, maybe more."

"No good," Mathiras says, watching the cluster of crates across the surface of the asteroid. Those were crates we'd found abandoned on the surface, and thinking that the ship in distress had offloaded its cargo, we'd started to take it on our ship.

Dumb. The szzt pirates caught us unawares and nearly blew a hole through our heads. Kaspar managed to fling a few of them aside and Adiron created enough cover fire for all of us to sprint over to our current hiding spot. Of course, we're about a hundred yards away from our damned ship, and pinned down.

"Try to send the *Sister* another remote command," Mathiras tells me. "See if we can get her out from under them, at least."

I pull up the ship's remote system controls on my wrist-comm. It blats at me angrily, just like it has for the last while. "They're still jamming us."

My brother grunts. "We'll think of something."

A shot zings out through space, making a whining noise as it zooms past, and Adiron grabs Kaspar by the collar, flinging him backward again. "Lean in, big brother."

"What if I rushed them?" Kaspar asks, a daring glint in his eyes.

"What if they shot a hole through your stupid head?" I counter. "What then?"

"You could have my oxygen filters," he tells me with a wink.

"I'm *going* to shoot a hole through your head," I mutter, even as another shot sizzles past. Kef it, this is just stupidity. "They're going to keep us pinned down until we run out of air and just help themselves to our gear."

"You got a better idea?" Adiron asks me.

"I wish."

"We'll think of something soon," Mathiras says, and Kaspar's practically itching to get out there, but he waits for the plan for once.

"We have to," I agree. "We—"

My personal comm chirps.

Everyone stares at me. I hesitate, because it's such a random, screwball thing to happen in a life or death situation. It can wait, of course. We're under fire and dangerously low on oxygen and—

The personal comm chirps again.

"You gonna answer that?" Adiron asks.

"Don't you think we're a little busy?" I hiss at him, even as the aliens across the way fire a few blasts in our direction once more, and we automatically duck.

"Might be important."

So's surviving, but when the personal comm chirps again, I glance down at it and tap to see who's sending messages. It's Sentorr. I feel a sharp stab of regret that I'll never get to talk to him again, because there's no way it looks like we're coming out of this alive. Another heavy rain of blasts hits the rocks and debris explodes in the air on us. We all duck, covering our helmets, and I feel a sting in one of my grav boots. I look down and there's a shard of rock sticking out near my ankle. Suddenly, it throbs and pain shoots up my leg.

I suck in a breath and reach down to grasp it, to pull the palm sized rock "stake" out of my leg.

"Don't touch," Mathiras warns me. "You'll break the seal on your suit."

I whimper, because I can feel blood starting to fill up in my boot. "I think it hit a vein. A big one."

"Just a little longer, Zo," Mathiras says, and looks over at Kaspar, who nods. Oh no. I know that look. That's the "we've got one last chance to save the day" look and it's going to involve a lot of risk for my brothers.

Before I can tell them not to move forward with their new plan, my comm chirps again.

"Will you just keffing answer that?" Mathiras snaps. I tap it impatiently, even as the szzt shoot at us again, and the rocky cliffs creak and groan. That's...not good.

"Zoey?" Sentorr's voice echoes, tinny, in my helmet.

"Now's not a good time," I bark back. The moment they realize my personal comm is on a different band than the ship, they're going to jam it.

"Take cover," he calls out, and then hangs up.

What...

I look up just in time to see the pale white underbelly of a ship fly low overhead, her guns descending. Mathiras curses aloud and in the next moment, he tackles me.

Sonic booms surround us as Sentorr's ship opens fire on the enemy. Rocks fly into the air around us and the low gravity of the asteroid makes them bounce away and smack against our thin suits. After that, it's deafeningly quiet.

I don't know how long I'm stunned and dizzy, but eventually I manage to smack Mathiras's heavy arm that's on top of me. He floats up slightly, and I realize he's lost the seal on one of his grav boots. In the next moment, Kaspar snags him by the belt and thumps him back down to the surface of the asteroid. I try to get to my feet, my ankles throbbing from the tight clasp of the grav boots. My head's ringing and I'm half deaf — I can't tell if my comm is chirping at me again or not.

All's quiet down on the surface. I look over at Kaspar, and his lips move inside his helmet, but I can't hear what he's saying. I tap the side of my helmet and nothing but static comes through. Shit. I've lost communications. I point at my helmet and make a hand gesture indicating I've got no signal, and he nods agreement, then points at something in the distance.

Off on a nearby cliff, the *Fool* has landed. As I watch, three big mesakkah—judging by the horn compartments for their helmets —bound off of the cargo dock and slap down to the surface as if magnetized, their grav boots kicking in. They hop from rock to rock, moving steadily downward, and I get to my feet, dread in my stomach as I realize what's happening.

We're being rescued.

Which is awesome.

Except I'm still human and now there's going to be no hiding it.

I try to stand up and the throb in my ankles—especially the one boot—feels worse. Wincing, I hobble forward as Kaspar—ever the risk taker—comes out from behind cover and moves up, gun in hand. The air is filled with dancing bits of gravel that bounce back and forth like a mini meteor shower, and I push them aside as I move behind cover once more. I don't know if we're safe or not, but when Adiron follows him, it's a good sign.

Mathiras taps my shoulder and points, indicating it's safe to move forward. I head after him, my steps sluggish. I'm feeling a little lightheaded, but I'm sure it's because I gave my brain a rattle when Mathiras landed on top of me. I tap my helmet again and notice that the others on the *Fool* are coming to meet us midway.

I swallow hard...and my suit suddenly lets off a siren. Less than one minute of oxygen. "Guys?" I call out, but my words are muffled and I remember that no one can hear me speak.

They hear my suit's siren, though. In the next moment, six pairs of hands are grabbing me and then I'm hauled bodily toward the nearest ship—the *Fool*—as everyone rushes to get me to safety before I asphyxiate.

I force myself to breathe slowly, conserving oxygen as they hurry me across the surface of the asteroid and into the *Fool*. The moments seem to tick past like hours. One. Two. Three. I bend over, leaning against Adiron as I wait for the hatch to close and the life support to stabilize. My lungs hurt and it feels like the air in my suit is getting too thin, but it might just be my panicked imagination.

"Move aside! Move aside," a sharp, familiar voice calls, and then hands are clawing at my helmet, triggering the release at the neck. It's pulled off of my head and fresh air rushes in around me even as Mathiras takes a step back and Sentorr pushes his way in front of me.

We see each other for the first time.

I stare at him, silent. Sentorr's more handsome up close than from far away. His presence is commanding, his posture erect as if he still sees himself as a soldier despite the fact that he's been out of the service since the war (or so he told me). He's taller than I recall, his horns so tall and spread that they seem as if they're touching the stars. His face is as lean and austere as I remember from the pictures. I gaze up at him with my heart in my eyes and watch that full, perfect mouth thin into a line as he looks down at me.

"You're Zoey, aren't you?"

"Surprise," I manage, still breathless. The throbbing in my wounded leg seems to be worse by the moment, but it's nothing compared to the throbbing of my even more wounded heart.

Sentorr looks me up and down. "This...explains much."

Before I can speak, Adiron grabs me around the neck and hauls me against him, noogie-ing my head. "I nearly shat my pants out there, Zo. I thought you were a goner." He runs his knuckles over my head, scraping them in my hair and making me wince and feel like a child.

"Can you not?" I hiss at him, trying to squirm out of his grip.

Others are taking off their helmets around us, and I look into the faces of the other mesakkah from the *Fool* before turning back to Sentorr. He's awfully quiet, his expression impossible to read.

Adiron just noogies me again. "This the one you have a crush on, Zoey? I thought he'd be prettier."

Oh my god, I'm going to die. "Go kef yourself, Adiron!" I elbow him in the ribs and I'm relieved when he wheezes in response. I manage to writhe out of his grasp, stumbling forward as I do. A sharp pain lances up my leg and I yelp.

Strong arms catch me before I pitch to the floor. I'm not entirely surprised to look up and see that I'm in Sentorr's arms, or that he's so gorgeous it makes my heart hurt. For some reason, though, he's fuzzy. I squint at him, trying to sharpen his handsome features.

He says something, but my brain is fuzzy and I can't make it out. I just shake my head. "I'm sorry," I tell him. "I'm so sorry."

Someone bellows something—it might be Kaspar—about blood everywhere. Blood. Huh. Someone's bleeding? My leg throbs in a silent reminder and I look down. The slag of rock piercing my suit has almost come free, and I'm standing in a pool of blood around my grav boots.

Well, shit. The bleeder's me.

Sentorr says something again, but my brain won't focus. Everything's creeping into darkness when he sweeps me into his arms and surges forward, and I figure if I die now, I can die of happiness.

I'm in his arms, after all.

5

SENTORR

I stare down at the small human in the *Fool's* med-bay,
my fists clenching and unclenching as I watch Tarekh
toggle switches and run diagnostics over Zoey. It seems impossible to think that there are human females out there smaller
than Cat, but to me she seems terribly small and far too fragile.
Her pale features are tiny, her hands delicate, and her teats are
strangely large despite the fragility of her frame. Distracted, I rip
my gaze away and focus on Tarekh.

"Quit burning holes into my back with your eyes," the big ugly
brute says, not even looking up from his datapad. "She's going
to live."

The breath I didn't know I was holding expels from my chest.
"She's hurt."

"Yeah, shrapnel pierced her suit in a few places. Nicked a big vein.
She's a little shy on blood, but luckily we don't have to wait for

the machines to synthesize the appropriate blood type for her. Cat's the same type."

That explains why Tarekh's small mate has been hovering around, then. She pushed her way in past Zoey's three large brothers as if she belonged in the med-bay and no one stopped her.

Brothers. Ha.

I knew their faces long before I knew hers. Mathiras, Adiron, and Kaspar va Sithai, from the va Sithai family back on Homeworld. All three served in the war, and now all three have slid to the wrong side of the law, as so many have after the peace talks were dissatisfying to those that served and gave their blood, sweat, and youth to the harsh mistress of war. They have a sister, I know. I just never looked in the records to see that the sister was mesakkah.

I never thought that they'd have a human on their ship, much less one running the bridge.

As I watch, Cat sits down in a chair next to the bed that Zoey's slight figure is upon. She extends her arm and Tarekh slides a needle under her skin and caresses her cheek as he hooks the other needle into Zoey's arm to begin the transfusion.

It's utterly silent. Her brothers wait nearby, not speaking. I know if I look over, I'll see their accusing faces. They act like it's my problem that she's human.

"So...you look upset," Cat chimes in when it gets quiet. "You want to talk about it?"

"To you?"

Tarekh gives me a flat look. "Watch it, friend."

I nod, my mouth settling in a thin line. "That was ill-mannered of me. I'm just...worried." I scrub a hand down my face. "Tell me again that she'll be fine, Tarekh."

"Why do you care?" one of the brothers asks, and I turn to face him. It's the one that scrubbed his hand over her silky brown hair and held her under his arm like any brother would a mischievous little sister, the one with the big features and smile. Adiron. He's not smiling now. The look on his face is downright protective.

"I care because I love her," I tell him flatly.

"She's human," the tallest of the brothers says. Mathiras.

"Do you think I care?" I snap at him, turning to look back at Zoey's face. The moment the words leave my mouth, I know them to be truth.

I was shocked to see that she was human, of course. It wasn't what I expected. In fact, when the helmet was first pulled off of her, I had a heart-wrenching moment in which I thought we'd somehow rescued the wrong crew off the asteroid and that my Zoey was still out there somewhere in danger.

It took a moment for it to register that Zoey was the pretty young human woman in front of me.

Of course, now that it's sinking in, it all makes sense. Her self-imposed exile on the *Sister,* always staying behind when her brothers went out. Her strange name. Her refusal to send me pictures or establish a visual comm, even though we were clearly attracted to one another. She thought I would hate that she was human. She thought I would be upset.

I *am* upset. I'm upset that she withheld the truth from me.

I'm upset that she's lying in med-bay with Cat's blood being trans-ferred into her.

I'm upset that we've wasted so much time being apart.

I'm not upset that she's human. I don't care. She could be szzt. She could be krakenoid. She could be anything and I would love her because she's Zoey, and she's always been mine.

"You dickheads are shouting," Zoey murmurs from the bed, her voice cracked and raspy with sleep. "Can you not?"

Her brothers rush forward. I do, too, beating them to her bedside so I can loom over her. One elbows me as I put my hands on the edge of the mattress, leaning closer. I ignore him. "How do you feel?"

She licks her lips and gives her head a little shake as if to clear it, her eyes closed. She doesn't look at me. "I'm alive, and that's good enough." She turns away and looks over at her brothers, as if glancing past me, and smiles at them. "It's fine."

"It's not fine," I growl. "What were you doing there?"

Zoey lowers her gaze to the bed, toying with the blankets. "Answering a distress call, of course. I guess you're wanting a thank you. So...thank you."

Her tone baffles me, as does the lack of eye contact. It's like she's trying to avoid me despite the fact that I'm literally an armspan away from her bed. "Are you...angry? Zoey? Why won't you look at me?"

"Because I can't." She stares stubbornly at the blankets, picking at them.

Adiron gives my shoulder a shove. "Leave our sister alone. If she doesn't want to look at your ugly face, she doesn't have to—"

"Adiron," Zoey says sharply. "You're not helping."

I straighten and glare at her three hovering brothers. "Can everyone give us a minute? Zoey and I need to talk."

I expect them to protest, or for Zoey to say something cutting. It gets quiet in the room and Zoey just picks at the blankets for a long moment, silent. Then, she nods. "It's okay, guys."

"You sure?" Mathiras crosses his arms over his chest and glares. "We can go back to our ship at any time and—"

"I'm sure," she says quickly, trying to sit up in the med-bay bed. Off to the side, Tarekh adjusts the bed with the touch of a button, and then she's sitting up. With a quick caress of his mate's hair, he leaves med-bay, grabbing one of Zoey's brothers and dragging him along. The other two glare at me and slowly leave the room.

It's quiet, and I look over at the only other person remaining, Cat. She gives me a hint of a smile and holds out the arm still hooked up to Zoey, the blood transfusion still going. "Just pretend like I'm not here."

I grunt, because I don't want her in here, but Zoey needs the blood. I turn to my human, hating how small and fragile she looks in the bed. A thousand things bubble up inside me—frustration, anger, fear, joy...more frustration. I think of her brothers, clawing that helmet off of her so she won't die. I think of the fear I've been living with as we rushed to her end of the solar system to intercept the pirates. I think of all the times I imagined her dead in the last few hours and my gut churns.

I think of the way her soft hair curves around her face, and how beautiful she is. How could she think I wouldn't love her? "You should have said something," I murmur when I find my voice.

"About the pirates?" She tugs on a bit of the plas-film blanket, worrying it with her nails. "Well, if we would have known they were pirates, we'd have gone in a bit more prepared."

Her answer both amuses and exasperates me. She still would have gone in, but she'd have prepared more. Typical fearless

Zoey. "I wasn't referring to the pirates. I was referring to you being human."

Zoey's gaze flicks up to me, her eyes narrowing and her forehead pleating in a way that's fully human. "What am I supposed to say about that? Sorry I'm so gross and human?"

Gross? I'm shocked. Does she truly think I'd find her repulsive? When she stares down at the blanket covering her hips again, worrying the minute tear in the plas-film, I realize that's exactly what she thinks. "Why won't you look at me, Zoey?"

"Maybe I don't want to see the disgust on your face," she says, gaze averted. "You've made it quite clear how you feel about humans."

Cat clears her throat, trying to hide the smirk on her face.

I bare my teeth at her. "What did I say that makes you think I find you 'gross,' Zoey?"

"Come on, we both know you don't like humans. You've made it quite clear that you don't understand the others and their relationships with their mates." She looks over at Cat. "Sorry."

"No big. He doesn't hide it from us, either." Cat doesn't look offended, though, just amused. "You should hear his bitching when one of us decides to have a date night—"

"No one asked you, Cat," I snarl.

"See?" She tilts her head and gives me a smug look.

Zoey just shakes her head, and she looks so sad that my heart aches. "You're angry. I knew you would be. That's why I kept it secret for so long."

My head feels as if it's exploding. "I *am* angry," I manage. "I'm angry because you almost died. You're here in med-bay, bleeding.

You avoided me on the station and you won't even look at me right now. I hate that you came so close to death when you should have never been there in the first place. You should have been back on 3N, waiting to meet me—"

She looks up at me, shocked. "You think I could meet you? Ever? Looking like I do?"

"Beautiful?" I ask.

Now Zoey's the one that's confused. "W...what?"

I take her hand in mine, stopping her from fretting the blanket any longer, and sit on the edge of the bed. I look down at her knuckles. She has four fingers (and a thumb) where I only have three. She's small and pale where I'm blue, and my hand is nearly twice the size of hers. I run my thumb over her skin. It's different, but not unpleasant. "I told you that I never cared how you look. Nothing has changed. I feel the same way I do about you right now that I did a week ago, or a month ago."

She blinks at me, and her eyes are big and green and soft, her lashes thick. Her lower lip—pink and full—wobbles slightly. "And how is it that you feel about me?"

"You know how I feel."

The fire returns to her, just a little. Her jaw clenches and she looks so adorably stubborn that it makes me want to drag her into my arms and hold her tight. Her hand tugs at my grip. "Yes, well, I want to hear you say it."

I glance over at Cat, who's watching us with wide, gleeful eyes. This will be all over the ship in a matter of hours...and I find that I don't care. Let the entire universe know how I feel about Zoey. I hold her hand tightly and rub her knuckles. "I love you," I tell her plainly. "I will say it like a human and say I love you. I will say it like a mesakkah male and tell you that you have my heart. Either way, know that nothing has changed and I want you now as much as I ever have."

Her lower lip trembles, her eyes shiny with emotion. "You should know I'm a virgin," she blurts. "Like, super virgin."

I stare at her, unable to process what she's saying. It takes a moment to sink in, and I wonder if this is another thing she suspects will drive me away? "I do not care, because from this moment forward, you are mine."

"Wow, so this is getting awkward," Cat says, reaching over and tapping the "call" button over Zoey's head. "I'm going to bring the others in before you two start making out in front of me. Unless it's blood loss that's making her blurt these things out."

I just bare my teeth at Cat.

"I need to hear it again," Zoey says, squeezing my hand. "Before my brothers come back."

"I love you," I tell her, pressing my mouth to her skin. I have seen the others kiss and caress their mates without a plas-film protection, and at the time I thought it was vulgar. Now, though, I see the appeal. I don't want anything keeping me from touching Zoey. "You are my mate."

She smiles widely, showing square white teeth instead of mesakkah fangs, and I think she's still the most beautiful thing ever. "Really?"

"Really," I say. A split second later, her three brothers pile into the room.

"Break it up, break it up," Kaspar says, even as Adiron hauls me physically away from her. Mathiras moves to his sister's side and takes a protective stance, and for the moment I am pleased they are so very protective of her—and frustrated, too.

"It's okay, guys," Zoey says, calmly waiting as Tarekh moves to her side and checks the blood transfusion.

"He was touching you," Adiron growls. "He doesn't get to do that until we approve."

Zoey makes an exasperated sound. "Come here, Adi." When the big guy leans in, she flicks a finger on his plated forehead. "I get to make that call, not you."

"You are our sister," Mathiras says, putting a hand between the two of them before Adiron can rub his knuckles over Zoey's head again. He steps between the siblings and then looks over at me. "If you want to touch Zoey, you have to court her first."

"In human ways," Kaspar adds with a scowl.

"Human ways?" I ask, baffled.

"Yes. Like in the Earth vids she always watches."

Zoey just moans and claps a hand to her forehead. "Guys, for kef's sake."

"No, Zoey," Mathiras says, unyielding. "You're human. If he wants to be with a human, he needs to confront it. He courts you, human-style. That's all there is to it."

"It's easy," Adiron says, casting a sly look over at Zoey. "They like dumb shit. We know. We've lived with her for ten years."

She shoots him the finger, an expression I've seen Fran do to Kivian many times. It takes everything I have not to bark with laughter. Instead, I manage to keep my lips pinched tight and give them a solemn nod. "Then you'll let her stay on the *Fool* for now?"

Because it's just occurred to me that they could easily snatch her away. They could take her back on the *Little Sister* and head off and we'd be on separate ends of the galaxy for gods only know how many months. My chest tightens at the thought. I can't let that happen. I don't want Zoey out of my sight ever again. The thought's a painful one.

The three brothers exchange a look. "We'll figure something out," Mathiras says, and pats Zoey on the shoulder. "You rest for now, here with the medic."

"Oh, but I want to talk to Sentorr—"

"No," Mathiras says, and I find myself flanked by the two big brothers again. "He's coming with us."

"Uh oh," is all Zoey says. But I think she's grinning.

I find myself smiling, too. It's impossible not to.

6

SENTORR

*Z*oey's three mesakkah brothers drag me from med-bay down the hall. I don't even mind. I'm grinning to myself, thinking of my female and how she's truly, finally going to be mine. I think of her soft pale skin and her soft brown hair and—

Adiron slings an arm around my neck, nearly choking me. The guy is keffing enormous, almost as big as Tarekh and far more hands-on. "So. We need to talk."

"Leave him alone, Adiron," Mathiras says. He moves toward the docking bay of the *Fool,* then pauses and crosses his arms over his chest again. "Our sister is in love with you." It's a statement, not a question.

I nod. "We've been talking for months. I didn't know she was human, and I don't care. She has my heart."

"So if we leave her here with you for a few days, you'll look after her?"

"We're leaving her here?" Adiron scowls at Mathiras. "What the kef—"

Kaspar reaches over and smacks the back of Adiron's head. "Think, you big dummy. How are we going to hunt down the rest of the pirates if Zo's hurt and in danger? This way she's out of the line of fire."

Adiron just scowls at him, rubbing the back of his head. "I guess."

Mathiras watches me with intense scrutiny. "You tell Zoey we're just finishing our run. She doesn't have to know that we're going after the mother ship in case there's other pirates."

I nod. "Because she's going to want to go after them as well?" The thought of her flinging herself into danger makes my blood run cold. "You have my word."

"Zoey will be safe with you," Mathiras says. "Your other humans seem to be happy. That's enough for me, for now."

I'm a little surprised. "You're trusting her to me?"

"No, we're trusting Zoey to Zoey," Kaspar says, and for a moment, he looks as if he wants to smack me on the back of my head. "She's a tough little scrapper, and smarter than most give her credit for. She can look after herself, and if you don't believe that, you don't know Zoey as well as you think."

Adiron grins. "And if you piss her off, she'll have your balls in a vise."

"You care for her greatly." I'm impressed at their faith in their human "sister."

"She's a hard little shit to love, but once you do, you'd kill for her."

Mathiras gives me a crooked grin. "We'll be back in a week or so. I expect you to let her set the pace."

Is he lecturing me on mating? I don't know what to say. "Of course," I manage stiffly.

"And make sure that medic takes good care of her."

I narrow my eyes at him. "Now you're insulting me if you think I'd let her get further injured."

"She's human in a mesakkah world," Mathiras says bluntly. "I know that. You know that. Sometimes Zoey forgets it, though. She desperately wants to be mesakkah. We treat her like she's mesakkah. But deep down, she's not. She's as fragile as any human, and sometimes she forgets that. I'm just saying...be careful with her."

"Or we'll come back and tear your throat out," Adiron says cheerfully.

ZOEY

Pretty sure the ugly bastard running the med-bay slipped a mickey into my transfusion, because I fall asleep before my brothers and Sentorr return. When I wake up later, the lights are dim with the ship's version of "nightfall" and it's all quiet. Someone's pulled back some of the paneling to reveal a window out to the stars, and it's all quiet, nothing but empty space and endless stars around us.

No asteroid.

No *Little Sister*.

I sit up abruptly, my head swimming. "Mathiras? Kaspar? Adiron?"

A large figure emerges from the shadows on the far side of the room, and I suck in a breath at the sight of him. It's not one of my brothers, but the man I've been having filthy dreams about ever since I first heard his voice. "Sentorr."

"Your brothers are gone," he says, his voice crisp and yet somehow sexy with authority. "They went on with the passengers on the *Little Sister*. You're to recuperate and stay here...with me."

Even though he stands tall and erect by my bedside, there's an odd glint in his eyes that makes me shiver. He's watching me like...like Adiron watches his favorite bowl of noodles, or the way Kaspar gets that look in his eyes when there's a dangerous sort of job calling his name.

No one's ever looked at me like that before, like they want to devour me whole.

I keffing love it.

I fight the urge to squirm in the bed, because I'm still a little sore and achy. My leg throbs and I'm tired—and yet wired at the same time. "I can't believe they left me here." I'm a little shocked by it. It's the first time my brothers have left me behind in the ten years I've been with them. I'm also a little hurt. "They don't need me?"

"I'm sure they do. But I won't let them take you while you're injured. I can keep you safe here." He gazes down at me in that stiff manner for a moment longer, and then sits on the edge of the bed again, taking my hand in his. "You're safe with me, Zoey. No one is going to hurt you."

I nod. On one hand, it's a little terrifying because this is the first time I've "flown the nest" as Earth people say. Every day of my life has had one brother or another in some sort of supervisory fashion. If Kaspar and Mathiras went on a mission, Adiron stayed with me. They'd switch out "sister watching" duties so I was always protected. But now I'm here alone on the *Fool* with the man of my dreams. I shiver and I don't know if I'm scared or excited.

He takes my hand in his, caressing my knuckles and gazing down at our joined fingers.

I decide the shiver is excitement.

Sentorr's so quiet I feel like I have to say something. "I saw you, you know. On Three Nebulas."

He looks up at me, surprise on his sharp, austere features. "When?"

"You passed me on the walkway. I had a holo concealing my features." I grimace a little. "I always pose as Vanora va Sithai when we go out so no one asks questions. Most of the time, though, I just stay on the *Sister*. It's easiest."

"Humans aren't widely accepted," he agrees, still playing idly with my fingers in a way that makes my nipples tighten and my pulse thrum low in my belly. "I know the others are especially protective of their mates when they go out on stations. The women wear collars so people think they're pets."

"Oh, that's clever. I never thought of that."

"It's demeaning," Sentorr says flatly. "They deserve better."

"Yeah, well, there's an Earth saying—shit in one hand, get what you deserve in the other, see which fills up faster." Okay, so it's not exactly like that, but the message should be clear enough.

He just snorts, his fingers lightly caressing the bumps of my knuckles, especially my pinky. "Truer words never spoken."

"I'd rather wear a slave collar than a holo," I admit. "A holo makes me nervous. If it fails, I'm totally exposed. A slave collar just makes everyone ignore me."

"I wouldn't want you to wear one."

"Yeah, but...would you treat me like a slave? Pull my hair and make me call you daddy?" The words are supposed to be teasing, but they come out all soft and trembling because I'm terrible, terrible, terrible at flirting. Part of me is shocked by what I'm saying and part of me is thrilled at the boldness of it all.

Sentorr's eyes meet mine and he holds me pinned there by the force of his gaze. "I would treasure every inch of you."

That small, fervent statement steals the breath from my lungs. "Gosh, is it hot in here?"

Immediately, his hand goes to my forehead. "You're feverish?"

"No, just being a dork," I admit, wondering if it's all right to grab him by the collar of his shirt and haul him down against me for my first kiss. Too soon, I wonder? Because I want to kiss him more than I want anything. "So...what does this mean, you and me? Where do we go from here?"

To my surprise, a hint of a smile touches his face and I can feel myself smiling back, utterly enamored. I thought my three brothers were good-looking (even Adiron in his dopey sort of way), but Sentorr puts them to shame. There's such stern nobility in his features that it makes me want to strip him naked and do bad, naughty things to him to crack that hard facade.

He leans back, his hand moving away from my brow. Instead, he tucks the blankets tight around my body. "Tonight, you sleep in med-bay and recover. Tomorrow, I start courting you."

"Courting me?" I'm not entirely sure I heard him correctly.

"Your brothers insist. If I am to claim you as mine, they want me to woo you like humans woo their females. So I am going to leave here when you go to sleep, and I am going to ask Fran and Iris and Cat how one courts a human female."

I don't know if I'm thrilled that my brothers told him to do that, or annoyed. I kind of want to jump his bones. I'm not sure where that fits in the courting scheme of things, but I also know I'm impatient. Courting might be fun. "Will you hold my hand and talk to me until I sleep, then?" I ask, snuggling down on the blankets.

"If you want it."

"I do. I don't want you to go," I tell him softly, and bite back the "ever again" that's brimming on my tongue. I'm an intense sort of person and I should probably give him a day or two to ease into the idea. He knows me, but he doesn't *know* me.

Best to not scare him too much yet.

He touches my hand and sits next to the bed, and I'm content...for now.

7

ZOEY

*W*hen I wake up, Sentorr's not in med-bay. I guess he can't wait around holding my hand forever, but I'm still a little sad. I yawn and rub my face, and before I can get up, one of the human women bustles in. She's tiny, even for a human, and I doubt she's within spitting distance of five feet tall. This is the one that gave me blood—Cat. For a moment, I just stare at her because it's so very…odd to see someone with human features wandering around. For so long, I've seen nothing but handsome blue mesakkah faces, and other, far less attractive alien races. Cat's smooth brow and lack of tail is a little shocking to see and yet makes me weirdly homesick at the same time.

"Hey there," she says cheerily. "Tarekh will be in after a moment to check on you. How are you feeling?"

"I'm fine," I tell her and casually shift the plas-film blanket aside, peeking at my leg. The gash must have been pretty deep, because despite the surgical machines on the ship, I still have a pink, dimpled spot on my leg where the flesh has knitted but not entirely returned to normal. "It's nice to finally meet you. Sentorr's told me a lot about the crew here." Of course, he only recently told me that half of them are human, but I leave that part out.

She looks over and gives me a wry expression, even as she picks up something that looks like a dirty sock off the floor. As I watch, she moves around the small med-bay cabin, tidying up and collecting bits of strewn clothing, recyclable noodle containers, and what look like spare parts for the ship itself. "We live with Sentorr. You don't have to soft-pedal it for our sakes. We know he can be a real pain in the ass."

"He said Tarekh's a slob and that you give him shit all the time," I admit, grinning.

Cat preens a little. "That might be the nicest thing anyone's ever said about me."

Tarekh enters the room and he gives his smiling mate a hot look that makes me feel a little awkward—and a little jealous. He caresses her cheek as she picks up a discarded shirt and then moves to the machines monitoring me. "Let's take a look at how our patient is doing."

"I'm fine," I tell him and do my best not to seem too eager. "Can I go to the bridge and see Sentorr?"

"He's not going anywhere," Tarekh says, punching buttons on the med-bay equipment. "I need to do a few scans to make sure you're all right, and then I'll release you. Cat will show you to your room."

"My room?" I blink at the thought. Of course I'm going to have a room. It's not like they're going to let me sleep in the cargo bay or something. It's weird though...I never thought of being on the *Fool* and not sharing a room with Sentorr. But maybe he doesn't want me to. Wait, what if he's had time to think about things and changed his mind? What if all he wanted was a long-distance relationship and now that he's had longer to stare at my human face, he's having doubts? Chewing my lip, I wait for Tarekh to finish.

"It's less of a room and more of a closet," Cat admits. "We're low on space on board, but we've cleaned out one of the storage compartments and put a cot in there. I hope that's all right. It's cozy and secure if not exactly spacious."

"It's totally fine. Sentorr mentioned that quarters were tight on the ship." Oh boy, and now I'm that dork that mentions the guy she's crushing on all the time. When Tarekh smirks at me, I know I'm right and I force myself to be silent.

The big medic unhooks the monitors from my arm. "Looks like you're all right, just take it easy today and try and stay off the leg." He turns away from me and leans down to give Cat an affectionate peck on the mouth. "She's all yours now, love."

She gives him a flirty look and then furtively caresses his tail when he turns away, and the big man jumps. She only giggles and flutters her eyelashes at him, and now I'm filled with envy at their silly, affectionate relationship. "Come on, Zoey. Let's get you some clothes. We bribed a tailor back at Haal Ui to make some human "costumes" and we've got a decent-sized wardrobe. I'm sure we can find something that fits you."

Bribing a tailor? Clever. I never thought to do that. Of course, I never went around as human, either, so it wouldn't have mattered. "Thank you."

Cat leads me away and through the ship, pointing out rooms as if I don't know the layout of the *Fool* by heart already. Sentorr told me that she was a Class IV Private Cruiser from Homeworld and I downloaded schematics and carefully filled them in from our conversations, like the obsessed stalker fangirl I am. I know that Sentorr's the only one with a room to himself at the moment. I know Fran and Kivian share the largest room, since Kivian's the captain. Alyvos and Iris are across from Sentorr, who has the smallest chamber. He's said before that he doesn't mind having the smallest cabin because it reminds him of his days back in the military, when he had to bunk with four other men in a closet-sized room while stationed on a terraforming planet. Now that I'm here, I wonder if that's why he wants me to have my own room…or if it's because he needs space to get used to the idea of me.

The reality of being face to face with each other changes everything, I realize that. I just hope that he doesn't change his mind about me.

Cat leads me down the hall, and at the end is a door marked "storage" in Mesakkah Proper, the written language used on Homeworld and in all legal documents. She gives me a little grimace of apology then opens the door.

Inside, though, it's charmingly cute. Decorative art has been hung on the walls and expensive, synth-silk scarves drape over storage boxes. Just as promised, there's a small cot in the corner, but festive, colorful blankets and a multitude of pillows cover the bed. Iris sits on one corner, a vivid purple ribbon over her eyes, and Fran, Kivian's mate, stands nearby folding something fabric into a box. They turn as the door opens and Fran's pretty face widens in a smile. "Welcome! I hope you're feeling better."

I smile at her. "I am, thank you." I can't stop staring. Cat's cute in an impish, wholesome sort of way, but Fran's beautiful. She's got long black hair, dark eyes, and smooth golden skin that could point to a variety of ethnicities. Iris is more elegant than lovely, with wavy dark hair and a gentle smile.

They're all so different and so *human* that I get choked up at the sight of them together. My brothers have always protected me from the trafficking side of the galactic underworld, so seeing so many human faces in front of me is overwhelming. "Hi," I manage around the knot in my throat.

Fran gestures at the room. "I know it's not much, but we're not really a passenger ship."

"It's lovely. Thank you for making it so welcoming."

Iris just smiles, her face turned toward us. "Sentorr asked us to make sure you had a comfortable room. As if we'd let you sleep on the floor."

"We thought since we were here, we'd have a girls' day," Fran says brightly, taking my arm and steering me toward the cot. "Rumor has it that Sentorr's going to be dating you per your brothers' demands, so we thought we'd help you with hair and makeup and wardrobe."

I touch my hair. Since my three brothers were the only ones that ever saw me, I mostly kept it in a ponytail at my nape. I've never worn makeup, since I was only ten when I was taken. The thought of making myself pretty for a date is probably silly, but it's also wildly appealing. "If you don't mind..."

"Mind? Girl, we've been looking forward to this all day." Fran takes me by the arm and pulls me toward the cot. "You sit next to Iris. We're going to make you irresistible to him."

Iris touches my hand as I sit down. "Can I braid your hair?"

"Sure?"

"I'll be in charge of makeup," Fran says. "Cat, you do wardrobe. This'll be like one of those makeover shows. You ever watch those, Zoey? With the right transmitters, you can sometimes pick up satellite feeds from Earth. Did you know they started *Queer Eye* again?"

I'm mostly silent, listening as they chatter around me. Iris's fingers are gentle as she deftly and expertly braids my hair, and Fran seems to hold up more eyeshadow to my eyes than she actually puts on me while Cat picks through clothes and chats. It's clear they all know each other well and that they're comfortable in their place on the ship. It's nice to see that they act like any other normal human girls instead of downtrodden slaves, but at the same time, I feel weirdly left out. I know more about navigation systems and the best route to save fuel than what color of eyeshadow would go well with my eyes.

"So, I need to bring this up," Cat says, holding a light blue shimmery floral tunic out to me. "Do you, uh, know about mesakkah anatomy?"

"You mean the spur?" I close my eyes while Fran dabs something on my lids. "Yeah. I've seen my brothers naked. When I was little I used to unlock the lavatory door and jump in and scare Adiron all the time."

"That's one less shock for you, then," Fran says, amused.

"You should also know that they really like their tails touched, and the underside of the spur is sensitive," Cat chimes in.

"And they don't know what a clit is because female mesakkah don't have them," Iris says. "So if he doesn't give you the right touches, make sure you point that out to him."

This is rapidly getting awkward. "You guys really think Sentorr wants to have sex with me?"

"I think if he doesn't, he'll die of blue balls," Cat says. "I saw the way he was looking at you."

"Tell me more about him," I say eagerly, clutching the tunic to my chest. "I know him through our conversations, but you guys know him in a different way."

"What do you want to know?" Fran asks.

I sigh happily. "Everything."

FOR THE NEXT TWO HOURS, the girls fill my head with tales about Sentorr. They share stories of visits to dangerous worlds for odd jobs, cantina brawls, and even stories of back when Sentorr served in the military before turning to a life of piracy at Kivian's side. It's clear that the crew gets along like a family—that despite the occasional spat, they have each other's backs.

Fran worries he's too serious.

Cat thinks he works too much.

Iris thinks he's lonely.

I think they're all right, and it makes me want to grab him and kiss him until he smiles. I want to hold him close at night and smother him with love. I want to be there for him when he's feeling lonely and sad. I want to talk star charts with him and discuss the fastest way around a nebula.

I want everything.

Once my hair is braided into a tight tail that starts above one ear and moves across my head like a half crown, Iris gives me a pat, indicating she's done. I change into the clothes Cat gives me and Fran finishes my makeup with one last dusting of brushes, and then they leave. I'm to meet Sentorr in fifteen minutes in the mess hall, and everyone's going to give us privacy so we can have our "date." I think they might be more excited than I am.

After they go, it's quiet, and I fiddle nervously with the hem of my tunic.

I feel...odd. Not like myself. The tunic and pants are completely different than my normal jumpsuits. I usually dress just to cover my limbs and for convenience. I've never worn anything...pretty. This is girly and feminine, with a light shimmer to the blue fabric and artful cutouts on the long sleeves. The flower pattern seems to shift colors as I move, and the fabric flows and drapes and clings, especially to my breasts. I feel exposed. On a whim, I get up and sneak out of my "room" and down the hall to the lavatory. In there, I get a look at myself in the mirror.

I'm...beautiful. I touch my face, because Fran's managed to make me go from blah human to startlingly pretty. My eyes are big and bold, my mouth is rosy and plump, and my cheeks and brows look perfectly defined. I can't stop staring at my features, both shocked and pleased. Sentorr's sure to love how I look now.

The moment the thought crosses my mind, I feel uneasy. Suddenly I don't like my reflection. The girl in the mirror is pretty and feminine, but she's not Zoey va Sithai. I shouldn't change who I am to impress Sentorr. He has to like me for me, humanity and all.

With a little sigh, I grab a towel from the stacks in the storage compartments, peel the sanitary wrapper off of it, and then begin to wipe my face clean of Fran's artistry. When the makeup's gone, I loosen my hair from Iris's artful braid, and then shake my brown, messy locks out and pull them into a low ponytail. I can't do much about the tunic, but I knot and tuck the long, flowing sides until they're less drapey, and then I look at myself in the mirror again.

My plain face stares back at me, my hair uninspired. Tucking in the tunic itself ruins the flowing lines and almost makes it look like one of my jumpers.

If Sentorr can't love this girl, I don't want him anyhow.

8

SENTORR

I adjust the cuffs on my sleeves, over and over again, as I wait for Zoey to arrive.

The mess hall has been cleared out and cleaned up. Pale white fabric has been draped over the main table, with two chairs set there. Cat told me I needed fresh-cut flowers for the table, but they're nowhere to be found, so Fran let me borrow a rare vizhii plant she keeps in the private quarters she shares with Kivian. Two places have been set, with two glasses of delicate ooli fermented brew and two bowls of noodles. It's perfect.

I toy with the cuffs of my best uniform again. It's one of my old military jackets, a bit outdated since I left Homeworld's forces over ten years ago, but it's the most dressy thing I own and Zoey deserves the honor of a date who cares about his appearance. I want to pace the room, but I don't dare, lest she show up in the next moment and see how nervous I am. I want her to be impressed by me. I'm not as sociable or attractive as Kivian, or as muscular as Tarekh. I'm not as good a fighter as Alyvos, but I still want Zoey to look at me with those hopeful, shining eyes like she did in med-bay.

I can't wait to see her, and eye the drinks bubbling in their crystalline glasses on the table. I'm nervous and could use a steeling drink myself, but I wait. She'll be here soon, I know, and chide myself for my impatience.

The door chimes and I straighten, going military stiff, hands clasped behind my back as Zoey enters the room. There's uncertainty in her eyes, but she still takes my breath away. She's wearing some feminine get-up that I've seen one of the other humans in before, which makes sense as her own clothing is currently being repaired and cleaned. Her hair is pulled back from her face, and all I can see are her fresh-scrubbed, pale cheeks, her green eyes, and her smooth brow that's devoid of horns. She stands perfectly still and looks at me. "Hi."

I gesture at the table. "Please be welcome to our human date, Zoey."

Her mouth twitches and she gives me a wry look. "You know back on Earth they just call it a date."

"Of course," I manage, my tone stiff and tight. I want to tell her that she is lovely, that it's taking everything I am not to reach out and caress her soft skin and learn her body with touches, but this is important. I move forward and pull her chair out, as Fran instructed me to do. This is part of the human ceremony of "date," I have been told.

Zoey fiddles with one of the strange knots on her tunic for a moment before surging forward and sitting down. "Thanks."

I push her chair in gently and then retreat to my side of the table, sitting across from her. It's utterly silent in the room, and it feels...

unnatural. Zoey and I have always been able to talk to each other easily, so I don't understand why she doesn't speak. I consider a million topics to bring up and then discard each one as stupid or unimportant...or inappropriate. As she gazes down at the food and drink set in front of her, I decide that's a safe topic. "Cat drank all of the human beers we had on board, so I'm afraid we only have ooli brew."

She wrinkles her nose. "I'm not a fan of beer or ooli brew. Got any night tea?"

Night tea is a mesakkah drink, one preferred by males that work long nights. It has a dose of adenosine receptors that's strong enough to knock a young mesakkah male on his ass, and I'm a bit surprised—and oddly pleased—that she likes such a plain drink. "I do." I get up and take the glasses of brew away, setting them on the mess hall counter before turning to the processor to brew two cups of night tea. "Are your quarters sufficient?"

"They're fine."

"I can trade with you if you like. You deserve better than storage."

"I don't want to take you out of your bed, Sentorr. It's cool." She goes silent and I turn to look at her. Zoey's watching me, thoughtful.

"What is it?" I ask.

"Nothing."

I take the cups of night tea and return to the table, and we both quietly begin to eat. Each time I stab my noodles, twining them on my utensil, I feel a bit more dismay. Where is our easy conversation? Where is the teasing Zoey I have lusted after for so long? Why is she so silent? I can feel my tail twitching with nervousness. I stir my noodles, my appetite gone, and look over at my dinner companion. The plant blocks much of her face, so I do my best to lean without being obvious, and catch a glimpse of her pink mouth pursed around a noodle as she eats.

My cock instantly hardens, and I look down again before I lose control. Kef me, that was a mistake. Did she truly think I wouldn't be attracted to her because she was human? I can't stop thinking about the softness of her lips and how they would feel against my own mouth...or lower.

"So."

I look up.

Zoey absently stirs her noodles, not looking up at me. "This is really awkward."

I nod slowly. "I admit I'm better on a comm channel than in person."

She grins, glancing up and her gaze meeting mine. "You're not the only one. I think I've been around my brothers for too long. I'm half-waiting for you to reach over and noogie my head, because Adiron always does that when I'm trying to eat."

"Noogie," I echo, and then remember his rough knuckle-drag over her hair. "Kef, no, I wouldn't do that. It looks like it hurts."

"That's the idea," she says with a little shake of her head. "He says it's too easy because I don't have horns." She goes silent and pokes at her noodles again. "I'm sorry I don't have horns. Or a tail."

"Horns are overrated," I find myself saying.

Her cheeks turn charmingly pink even as she smiles, and I'm fascinated. "Now you're just saying that to make me feel better."

"I am," I admit. "I don't think anyone's ever rated horns for them to be over- or under-rated."

Now she laughs and gives her head a little shake. "Tails, then."

"Tails are definitely important," I find myself teasing. "I suppose I will just have to overlook the loss and try not to let the shame of your tailless-ness overwhelm me."

Zoey blinks at me, and then snorts, grabbing a noodle and pitching it at me. "You and your tail can go kef yourself."

I laugh, pitching a noodle back at her. "I would, but you'd want to watch."

"Hell yeah I would." She slides my noodle into her bowl and then wiggles her eyebrows at me before giving it a vicious stab. "Pick up some pointers for my next conquest."

"Bah, there will be no next conquest." I can't tell if we're flirting or arguing. All I know is that it's fun and it feels more like Zoey than our awkward silence.

She grins, taking a drink of her tea. "You're overlooking my vast human charms. How many do you know can navigate a pirate vessel, fire a blaster, read and write four languages, and put up with mesakkah shit twenty-four seven?"

"Three," I say immediately, and she howls with laughter, pounding a hand on the table. I chuckle, too, utterly pleased at her amusement. I love making her laugh, love the carefree half-bark of it, as if she doesn't care who hears.

Zoey wags a finger at me, smiling, and then takes another gulp of her tea before giving me a speculative glance. "I've been meaning to ask you something."

My body tenses, and there's a hot throb in my cock again. I'm ready to confess exactly how I feel. How I want her naked and under me, exploring the differences in our bodies for hours before claiming her as my mate. "Go on."

"How did you get to 3N so fast? Did you burn all your fuel trying to catch up to me? I had a good day's lead on you."

Ah. I bite back any disappointment I feel. "Not all the fuel. Just three quarters of it."

One of her mobile brows goes up, a look I find charming and odd at once. "Bullshit. How?"

"I picked an alternate route." I pick up my tea and give her an arch smile. "Can you guess it?"

Her eyes gleam with my challenge and she leans in.

9

SENTORR

*T*alking to someone for hours has never been so pleasurable. Talking to Zoey over the comm has always been enjoyable, of course, but in person, I can see her eyes light up with enthusiasm. I can see the mischievous gleam in her eyes when she talks about outrunning a szzt freighter after robbing it. I can watch the movements of her hands as she tells a story about the time Adiron smuggled a dozen six-limbed wallats in their hold without telling Mathiras. I see the challenge in her face when she talks about her favorite routes and the best ways to save fuel, and the way she leans forward as she discusses recent changes in star charts, her breasts brushing against the table-top.

Talking ship has never been so keffing sexy.

Our night tea grows cold and the noodles go uneaten as I tell her about the time I spent in Homeworld's military service. Of how after two years of military action, I'd been stationed on a remote terraforming planet with only a handful of other people and how

I'd spent much of my time, alone and shuttling supplies between the different stations on the planet's surface and the bigger colony on the moon. It's where I'd learned to pilot and also grew accustomed to solitude. It's also where I met Kivian, who was stationed there for only about two months before the entire garrison was pulled.

Zoey tells me all about how her brothers rescued her, and some of their more dangerous smuggling runs, including one where a senator had to be removed from a blockaded planet. They'd nearly lost their lives on that one, and hearing the story makes me admire the bravery of the *Little Sister's* crew...and makes me want to deck her brothers for putting her in danger like that.

Eventually, she looks down at her empty mug and gives me a sheepish look. "I hope the others aren't expecting to get in here soon. We're hogging the mess hall."

I glance at the time. "I'm supposed to show you a vid after dinner," I admit. "A human movie, as part of the date."

"In your room?" she asks, brightening.

"No, the rec room."

"Ah." She thinks for a moment and then admits, "I'd rather go see the bridge."

"You would?" I'd rather go to the bridge, too, but I will endure some silly romantic human movie if it brings her enjoyment. I'll be happy just to sit next to her and watch her face.

"Yes! I want to see where you work." Zoey gets up from the table and moves to my side, grabbing my hand in hers and tugging me to my feet. "Come on. Give me the tour."

I'm entranced by that small, easy touch, the feel of her small fingers against mine. My body stirs in response and I force myself to think of unpleasant things even as I get to my feet. "How is your leg?"

"Hurts like a keffing bitch, but I can walk. It'll be good for me." She tugs on my hand again. "Don't try to get out of this."

I chuckle. "I wouldn't dream of it."

We leave the mess hall behind and I make a mental note to return afterwards and clean up. Right now, I'm not leaving Zoey's presence. I'm drawn to her like a planet to its star, trapped in the celestial pull of her radiance. She walks close at my side, looking at the ship with interest, as if mentally lining up what I've told her. I'm proud of the *Fool,* too, though I know she's an aging model and it'll be time to upgrade her at some point. She's served our crew well thus far, and I hope she has a few more runs in her yet.

As we get on the bridge, Zoey steps forward, her eyes lighting up. I let her head toward my station, content to watch her. The *Fool* has a small bridge, as she's a four-crew ship unlike the *Little Sister.* The *Sister* has a larger bridge for all that she has the same number crew, and a section for passengers. She burns a lot more fuel, though, and I like that the *Fool* can be efficient and speedy when she needs to be, whereas the *Sister* is more about brute force.

Zoey heads directly for my chair, her hands going to the headrest. She caresses it, and then slides into my seat, her eyes shining as she gazes on my station set-up. "This is exactly how I thought it would be."

"Is it?" Has she been imagining where I spend my time, then? I always picture her on the bridge as well, but I admit my thoughts are never entirely...wholesome. There's been many a night I've imagined her straddling me in my chair, or her ass pressed to the control panel as I rub my hand between her legs. Of course, in several of my visions, she'd been mesakkah, but now that I've truly seen her face, I find that it's all too easy to replace the old image with the new, better, true image of Zoey. Of soft brown hair and peachy skin and a delicate human build. I'm getting hard just thinking about it, but then again, I feel as if I'm always hard whenever I hear her voice.

I move toward my station, careful to conceal the bulge of my cock against one of the control panels. "What do you think?"

"I love it," she says softly, her gaze on the window out into space. "But then again, I love a ship and the stars. I love the openness of space and the potential it has. I love that there are endless opportunities for freedom if you only know how to take it." She looks over at me, smiling. "I think some of that is a leftover hang-up from when I was held captive as a child, but I love being a navigator. I love knowing that I can plot a course to anywhere and escape. That no one holds me back but me."

I nod, gazing out the window, trying to see what she sees. "I see duty. Responsibility to those I care for. My way to contribute." I glance over at her, unable to resist watching Zoey once more. "And far too much space separating me from you."

She looks over at me, breathless. Her lips part in surprise and she gets to her feet. I'm stunned that she's astonished. Haven't I shown her how much I care for her? Need her?

Clearly I have not shown her enough.

I put a hand on her waist, slow and deliberate, my gaze locked to hers so she knows exactly what I'm doing. Her green eyes are wide as she remains perfectly still. I pull her against me, tugging her forward until her breasts bump against my chest and I can feel her body against mine. Zoey looks up at me, and I can see anticipation and longing in her eyes. She wants my touch as badly as I want hers.

With my other hand on the back of her neck, I lean down...and down...and down, and gently brush my mouth against hers. Humans are short, but I don't mind. I'm finally kissing my Zoey. My mouth is on hers, in violation of every sanitary law on Homeworld and all its colonies, and I don't even care. Her lips are soft, and I'm stunned by the feel of them even as my arms go around her and I hold her close. I feel as if I have waited a lifetime to touch her.

And I know it's not enough. One kiss will never be enough. I want her everything.

Zoey makes an exclamation of pleasure in her throat at the kiss, and then she's pushing me into the navigator's chair and then straddling me like in every filthy dream I've ever had about her.

This is...unexpected. But good. So good. I'm panting as she settles herself over my lap, her thighs spread across mine, and she loops her arms around my neck. Groaning, I fight for control of the embrace. I want to show her just how much I need her. She can be in charge next time, but tonight she is mine. So I claim her mouth with a teasing, nipping kiss, thinking of all the things that the humans on the *Fool* have mentioned about kissing, because I want to please my Zoey. They use tongues. I remember that, and remember being appalled at the thought.

I'm not appalled now.

I'm greedy with hunger. I slick my tongue against the hot seam of her mouth, seeking entrance. I can feel her stiffen against me, her smaller body quivering as she straddles me, and my cock aches with need. I've never wanted anyone so fiercely. I swallow her little gasp of surprise, and this time when I stroke my tongue against her lips, she opens for me.

And now, I'm the one groaning. Her little tongue is slick and smooth against my ridged one, and the tangle of our tongues reminds me of mating. My cock aches, trapped under my clothing, but it can wait while I plunder the sweet heat of her mouth. I never realized until now why humans were so fascinated with kissing. I'm addicted to the taste of her, the feel of her lips, the soft darting of her tongue against mine, the noises she makes as she rubs against me. My hand slides to her hip, gripping her tight as she rocks against the iron-hard length of my erection.

For so long, I've waited for her. "My Zoey," I murmur between kisses, fighting to keep my caresses tender instead of overwhelming. I want her so much that it's difficult not to let myself go, to take everything she has to give like the selfish man I am.

"Oh wow, Sentorr," she breathes, her breath coming in soft little pants. She rubs her nose lightly against mine, her eyes sleepy with desire. "You're really good at kissing. Have you ever practiced?"

"You are the first one I have kissed," I admit to her, though I'm secretly pleased she finds my touch skillful.

"Me too," she admits. "I've never done any of this." Her hand slides down the hard wall of my chest, and she licks her lips, slightly swollen from my kisses. "You're...really big." And she reaches down between us and caresses the length of me through my clothing.

Everything in my body tenses. I bite back a snarl of need and put my hands gently on her shoulders. "Wait." I want her. I want her more than I have ever wanted anything, but her words are bringing me back to my senses. I know Zoey. She told me she has been with the pirate ship for the last ten years. Now that I know she's human, some of the pieces are filling in. "How old are you in human years, Zoey?"

"I'll be twenty-one in two months," she tells me, then leans in and bites lightly at my lower lip, tugging at it with her square little teeth.

I nearly lose control, because kef me, that feels amazing. She seems as eager as I am, her lithe body sending hungry, wild need through me. But I have to be smart. I have to be careful. Her brothers have entrusted me with her, and more than anything, Zoey trusts me. I won't abuse this trust.

I have to go slow and take care that she only feels hunger, that I don't scare her with the intense, possessive need I feel at the moment.

Because gods, do I want her.

"Slow down, Zoey," I murmur as she leans forward to kiss me again. "I want to make sure you're enjoying yourself."

"Are you kidding?" Her eager hands move over my chest, sliding up my pectorals and brushing over my nipples. "This is the most amazing, incredible feeling. I can't get enough of you. Are your nipples really this hard? I know my brothers have slightly different bodies than mine, but I've never touched their nips to find out. I want to touch yours." She tugs at the collar of my shirt.

"Calm," I tell her, capturing her hands before she can undo the fastenings on my clothing. "We don't have to mate right here on the bridge." And I press a kiss to the inside of one palm to ease the sting of my words. I keep kissing her, because I can't seem to stop myself. The skin of her wrist is so soft, so fragile. I lick it, feeling the heat of her against my tongue.

She shivers, her eyes full of desire as she watches my mouth on her skin. "I want you, Sentorr. Don't you understand? I've wanted you for so long. I'm tired of being patient. We're finally together. I want to do all the dirty things we've told each other." Her hand moves back to my cock and she strokes me again, so skillful that my breath catches in my throat. "Let me explore you."

Need wars with common sense. I want to touch her. Gods, I want to rip that pretty floral tunic off of her and shove my cock into her cunt and pump her full of my seed until she's screaming with joy. Even the mental image of that is so delicious that I nearly lose control, and I have to close my eyes. But I remember who I'm holding. My Zoey, who's hidden away from the world for ten years under one mask or another, because of her humanity. She's fresh and young and innocent.

I can't abuse that.

I kiss her again, and I keep it light and playful. When she whimpers against me, I break the kiss and stroke my thumb lightly over her cheek. "My Zoey. We have all the time in the world to get to know each other. Let us be patient a few days more."

"I'm not good at patient," she tells me, her pink lower lip thrusting out so prettily that I can't help but haul her against me to kiss her once more.

I'm not good at patient, either, it seems.

10

ZOEY

*W*hen Sentorr sends me back to my room that night with just a kiss and a promise to see me in the morning, it's clear that my gorgeous, sexy mesakkah hunk of a navigator is going to be honorable and take things slow.

Kef that.

I'm going to need to take things into my own hands. I lie in bed, cupping my throbbing pussy and know that touching myself to get off? Not gonna be worth it tonight.

Masturbating's great, don't get me wrong. But the real thing is down the hall and I want to touch him—and be touched—so badly that I'm aching inside in places I didn't know could ache. I slide my fingers down to my pussy, and I'm so incredibly wet and hot with arousal that I'm shocked. I've never turned myself on half as much as a few stolen kisses with Sentorr does.

Part of me loves that he's honorable. Part of me wants to show up at his doorstep, naked, and force him to lick my pussy. I don't think there'd be much forcing...but there'd be a hell of a lot of licking. Then I could do the same to him—tease him with my mouth until he got off.

That's...kind of going slow, right? No cock in pussy, so I'm sure that's slow by someone's terms.

I moan, my hands between my thighs, pressing on my mound as I contemplate my options. We can go slow, sure. We can also go slowly mad while honoring my brothers' wishes to have a real, honest-to-goodness courtship. Except my brothers don't seem to understand that I'm finally here with Sentorr. Courtship? What do they think we've been doing over the comms for the last few months? Trivia? Please. We've had the world's slowest courtship already—now that he's here in person, sexier than I ever imagined, I want to grab him with both hands and put my mouth all over him.

It's sweet of my brothers to think of my well-being, but they don't know the torture that the last few months have been, to be so deeply in love (and lust) with someone and think you can never have them. Now that I know I can have him? I'm tired of waiting.

I sit up on the bed, determined. I don't want to be alone tonight. I'm not scared or worried or shy—I'm turned on and I want the man I love to hold me and rub me in all the right places. I get to my feet and grab the pretty floral tunic. Everything's come unknotted, so I wear the drapes of it like a loose robe, tucking it around my body and not bothering to do up the ties. I grab my blaster, because I'm on a ship full of strangers, even if I trust Sentorr, and then open the door, peeking out into the hall. Deserted.

Good.

I tiptoe out of my room and shut the door quietly behind me, then move to Sentorr's door. The hall is silent, the only sound the whirr of air filters as they scrub the carbon dioxide from the ship's atmosphere. I go to Sentorr's door, and hesitate. Is he just going to send me away again? Protect me like my brothers have always been protecting me?

I glance down at the blaster in my hands and smile to myself. Not if I have a gun.

It might be a little extreme to hold my lover at gunpoint and demand he kiss me, but what do I have to lose? Nothing but my pride, I suppose. I pop the cartridge out of my gun and tuck it into the pockets of my tunic, since it's all clear.

Then, I knock quietly.

Before I have time to get nervous, the door opens. Sentorr's shirtless and disheveled, his normally military-perfect hair a tousled mess between his horns. He looks surprised to see me, eyes narrowing. "Zoey? What's wrong?"

I decide to grab the moment by the balls. "Pussy Patrol."

He blinks. "What?"

I turn the blaster on him. "Pussy Patrol," I repeat again. "We've heard rumor of unsatisfied pussy and have come to investigate."

Sentorr's lips twitch. "Is that so?"

"It is. If you'll step inside, please." And I flick the gun, indicating that he should move out of the doorway and let me in. When he hesitates, I nudge him with the end of the blaster. "Don't force me to take matters into my own hands, son."

I want him to smile, but all he does is step aside gravely so I can enter. I hope he's not upset at me or full of regret that I'm here and pushing things forward. I head into his room and I'm momentarily surprised at how very spartan it is. The bed's still made, with a few wrinkles mussing the blankets that tells me he was lying atop them. His walls are bare, with only a military plaque for service decorating the nearby desk. The door to his closet is closed, as is the adjoining lavatory, and the room is stark and bare and lonely. It makes me sad to see it and I forget all about my game—

—Until his hand closes over my wrist and he pulls the gun out of my grip. "What the kef are you doing here this late at night, Zoey?" He doesn't sound amused by my antics.

I turn to look at him, my hands going to my hips. "I wanted to see you. I wanted to kiss you. Hell, I wanted to sleep next to you. Is that a crime?"

"You should be in your room—"

"So my brothers can be satisfied knowing they've cockblocked their little sister even when they're not here? What about what I want?" I jab a finger into his chest. "Maybe I want to touch you. Maybe I want to have more than just a few stolen kisses. Maybe I've waited far too long to see you to just sit across the hall and twiddle my thumbs and—"

The words die in my throat because he tosses my empty blaster down on the bed and then cups my face in his hands. His mouth is on mine before I can think, and the world tilts around me. I lean into his kiss, the fierce, delicious caress of his lips against mine. I'm lost in him, in the slick of his ridged tongue as it drags against my own, teasing and plunging as if he's been waiting for this, too. There's such fierce hunger in him, in his kiss, that it makes my toes curl with want.

"Zoey," he murmurs between kisses, his breath warm and wonderful on my skin. "Just because I'm honoring your brothers' wishes doesn't mean I don't want you."

"How about you honor my wishes?" I fire back, biting at his lower lip. His horns are just out of reach, but man, I want to grab them so badly. "Or should I leave you to hook up with Kaspar or Adiron—"

He groans and then his mouth is on mine again, and the kisses get hotter and fiercer. I'm lost to the sensation of his mouth delving and nipping over mine, the drag of his tongue as he plunges into my mouth, the feel of his hands on my skin. He cups my cheeks a moment longer, and then his grip moves to my ass and he squeezes it tight, flexing his fingers. "I tried to be honorable," he tells me. "But kef it."

A little thrill shoots through my belly at his rough tone. "I don't want honorable. I want you to touch me."

Sentorr squeezes my ass again, and then he's lifting me into the air. I automatically wrap my legs around his hips, clinging to him as his mouth devours mine again, and the breath catches in my throat when his tail locks about my ankle, pinning me against him. Over and over, his mouth slants against mine, giving me hot, wet kisses that leave me breathless and distracted. And so good. God, his mouth is so good. I've dreamed of what it'd be like to kiss Sentorr, but I never imagined that it would make me feel this...lost, yet utterly possessed. Like the only thing anchoring me to this world is his fierce grip on my hips, or else I'd spin out of control.

His mouth hungry on mine, I barely notice that we've moved closer to the bed until the mattress is against my back and he rises up on his elbows. I whimper a protest, reaching to pull him back down over me, because I'm not ready for the kissing to be done. I might never be ready. Sentorr looks down at me, studying my face. "Pussy Patrol, huh?"

My cheeks flush. I feel exposed—and a little silly—now. "It was just a joke—"

"Is it? Because I'd hate for your pussy to be unsatisfied when I'm around." He lowers his head and gently nips at my chin, then moves to my neck, nuzzling against it.

His horn moves scarily close to my face, and I reach out and caress it with a sigh. It's covered in metal, so I know he can't feel my fingers, but I like touching them. I like learning him. I want to learn all of him. "I've wanted this for so long," I admit.

"Mating?" he asks, his mouth moving along my collarbone in a ticklish way.

"Touching you," I admit. "I didn't really think about mating at all until I met you. Then it made me want what I couldn't have."

Sentorr groans low in his throat and his face presses against my neck. "You never touched yourself?"

"Oh, all the time," I admit. "But I thought that was all I'd ever have. Now it feels like..." I break off, because I don't want to say it aloud. Masturbating's never going to be the same, not after kissing him. I have a sneaking suspicion it's not going to be enough ever again.

"Feels like what?"

"Nothing."

He lifts his head, eyes narrowing at me. "Don't make me force those secrets out of you."

Ooooh. "What are you going to do?"

"Everything. Anything." His hand moves over my collarbone, lightly brushing over the skin he just kissed, and then moves lower. I realize that my tunic-slash-robe is barely covering my breasts, and I suck in a breath, wondering if he's noticed the same thing. "Satisfy your pussy. Can't have the patrol coming after me."

I moan, because just hearing those words sends a pulse of heat between my thighs. I realize dimly that my legs are still wrapped around his hips, and I dig my heels into his butt, trying to drag him down against me. I want to feel his cock against my body.

Sentorr ignores the pressure of my legs, though, and his tail loosens on my ankle. Instead, he lifts his body off of mine until he's only caging me with his arms, and then reaches out and moves the loose fabric of my tunic aside, exposing one breast. I hold my breath, everything in me tensing as he gazes down at my bared skin. No one's ever seen me naked, not since I grew boobs and went from a flat-chested kid to a top-heavy adult female. I know they're bigger than they should be. Even the other humans on the ship don't seem to be as prominent in the torso as I am, and I wonder if he's going to be grossed out by it. Mesakkah women are all lean, elegant lines and muscle, with very little prominence to their breasts unless they're nursing. Me, I look as if I'm permanently nursing three very hungry triplets.

He continues to gaze down at me, saying nothing, and I bite my lip, doing my best not to move or jiggle anything. My nipple, already hard, grows tighter and more puckered under his gaze. "I'm sorry," I blurt out finally. "They're big, I know."

"Stop talking," Sentorr tells me.

"W-what?"

He looks up at me, and I can tell he's angry. "You're apologizing for your body. Stop talking if you're going to do that."

"Well, I know I don't look much like a mesakkah female," I begin, only to break off when he glares up at me once more.

"You think I want a mesakkah female? Still? After all we have been through?" He shakes his head. "I want you. I want you and your soft human skin and your brown hair and your big breasts and small body." Reverently, he brushes his knuckles over my nipple and I bite back a moan, because it feels even tighter and achier than before. "I find all of you perfect. And I like your big breasts."

"Oh, good," I say weakly. "Because I'm afraid they're not going anywhere."

He shoots me another look.

"Right. Stop talking."

"Correct. Now let me appreciate them without interruption." He lowers his head, and before his mouth can touch my skin, he looks up. "Consider this 'breast patrol.'"

Is...that a joke? I'm both surprised and amused and I want to tease him back, but then his mouth is on my nipple and I can't think of a damn thing. I lie flat on my back, stunned, my fingers clenching the blankets while he explores my breast with his lips. His mouth is soft and yet firm, moving over the rounded curve of my breast, teasing along the valley between them, and then finally moving back to the sensitive pink nipple. When his tongue brushes over it, the breath explodes out of my lungs and I reach up and clench his horns. "Sentorr!"

"Beautiful," is all he murmurs, rubbing his face against one breast before taking the nipple in his mouth again.

I'm a moaning, needy mess as he lavishes attention on my nipple, teasing the peak over and over before baring the other breast and then moving to give it the same consideration. I'm so aroused that my nipples feel as if they're made of diamonds, and my pulse is throbbing low between my thighs, giving me that strange hollow ache that's so new. "Please," I whisper, and I'm not even entirely sure what I'm asking for. Just that I want more of this...and yet it's still somehow not enough. When he lifts his head, my hips rock, involuntarily, and he gives one peak another hot, wet, open-mouthed kiss before starting to move lower.

"Breast patrol finds everything acceptable," he says in a low voice, and then dips his tongue into my belly button. "Time to satisfy the requirements of the Pussy Patrol."

That is the strangest—and most erotic—thing I've ever heard. Sentorr's playing my sexy little game in that stiff way of his, and I love it. I wriggle a little on the bed even as he slides lower, my open tunic now only covering my arms. The rest of it has fallen aside and I'm completely exposed to him. As he slides lower, I can't help but feel another stab of anxiety. Does my body match what he's anticipated? I know humans have hair between their thighs and mesakkah don't. I learned from watching human pornos that this is normal, though, and remember the shock and shame I felt in my youth when I started sprouting hair in awkward places, and boobs, and knew these weren't mesakkah things. It's hard not to think of that when he's sliding one of my legs over his big shoulder and gazing at my pussy with such intense scrutiny. After a few moments more, I can't stand it. "Say something."

He looks up at me, heat in his eyes. "Mine," he says thickly, and then his mouth is on me.

I gasp, because his face there is utterly shocking. I remain completely still as his tongue explores me with hard, hungry licks, pushing through my folds and delving into my core.

A ragged groan escapes him, shocking me with how needy it is. "You're so keffing wet, Zoey."

"Am I?" God, who is that breathless creature responding to him? It doesn't sound like me. It's too faint, too full of longing.

"You're covering my face with your honey," he tells me, and just hearing that makes me all jittery and needy. I arch my hips, then freeze, wondering if I should do that. But he only makes a sound of pleasure and then lowers his mouth to me once more.

And oh god, his tongue is everywhere, licking me and stroking me. I can hear how wet I am, hear his tongue moving over me, and it's somehow obscene and sexy all at once. I bite down on my knuckle to stop the little noises rising in my throat, because he's licking me everywhere and it's both fascinating and still not enough. He's avoiding my clit, and I remember idly that mesakkah women don't have one. That the inside of their cunt is ultra-sensitive whereas we humans have a pleasure button on the outside.

It seems a shame to interrupt with pointers when his mouth is so very nice, though. And it is good. I love his mouth on me, love the feel of his tongue and his lips, the nuzzle of his face against my inner thighs. I just won't come from this. And if this is going to be my first time having sex, I guess that's okay, too. I read somewhere that not everyone comes every time.

He gives my pussy another lingering lick, and then pushes my folds apart. "I see it now," he murmurs.

That makes me go up on my elbows to check, too. "See what?"

The look Sentorr gives me is smoldering and I swear my pussy's getting wetter just from eye contact. "I watched a human mating vid earlier so I would know how to touch you."

"You did?" If I had pearls, I'd clutch them. "That's so naughty."

"I wanted to learn your body so I'd give you pleasure," he tells me, and then takes one thick blue finger and slowly circles around my clit. "And I'm glad I did because I learned about this.

The one in the vid was pierced, though. It's harder to find without a little silver hoop attached to it."

I fall back on the bed with a choking gasp. That light touch felt as if electricity was rocketing through my body. Dear god. I've touched my clit tons of times on my own, and it's never felt half as intense as that one small caress.

"Ah, but it looks like my research has paid off," Sentorr murmurs in that sexy, delicious voice of his. "I've found the spot that will make you lose control, have I?"

I arch my back, panting. I love the dirty talk...but I also feel the overwhelming urge to grab him by the horns and shove his face back between my thighs so he can lick me until I come. "Sentorr," I beg shamelessly. "I need more."

"More touches?" And his blunt finger circles my clit again, making me nearly slide off the bed. If my hips weren't cradled inches from his face, I'd be on the ground already. "Or more of my mouth?" And he leans in, hot breath fanning over my skin.

"Yes please," I manage.

He chuckles, and the sound is so sexy that I moan all over again. "My beautiful Zoey," he murmurs. "I'm going to take my time. Wouldn't want the Pussy Patrol to give me a citation."

I'm on the verge of pointing out that the Pussy Patrol is a dumb thing I made up, and we don't give citations, but then he takes his thumb and rubs it up and down over the side of my clit, and I forget everything. I grab his horns and hold on as he touches me over and over, learning my body and describing it in great detail. How his fingers are dancing along the sides of my clit, or how he's rubbing it with the pad of his thumb. How he's going to sink one finger into my cunt and stretch me so I can fit his cock. How he'll lick every fold twice over and lap up all my juices. He tells it all to me in explicit detail and takes his time, so when he finally lowers his head and puts his mouth on my clit instead of just his fingers, I'm so primed that I scream, the orgasm exploding through me with the force of a supernova. Everything in my body ripples and clenches, and the climax shudders over my body like a wave. It feels so good that I keep rocking and moving with it and with Sentorr's mouth, only to realize that he's not going to let me come down from the climax. That he's going to keep licking and teasing me with his tongue, his lips and mouth on my clit, until I come all over again.

"Sentorr," I gasp, tugging on his horns. I need a moment to breathe, to relax.

"Not yet," he growls, hands locked on my thigh as he continues to drag his tongue over my clit, teasing me with those delicious ridges. "I haven't had my fill of you."

I want to tell him to stop, to wait, to let me have a breather, but then he suckles anew and I forget all about waiting. God, I want this and I want his mouth on me so bad. I dig my heels into his back, clinging to his horns as I grind against his mouth, crying out as the force of yet another orgasm begins to quake through me. If the last one was hard and fast, this one is languorous and takes so long to roll through my body that I'm practically crying with my second release. This time, after I come, I collapse on the blankets, panting, and gaze up at the ceiling, wondering if it's spinning or if it's just me.

My pussy throbs with how well it's been used, and I give a contented little sigh as he kisses the inside of my thigh. I feel... incredible. So good. That hollow ache in my belly isn't quite gone, but it's been overwhelmed by the mellow pleasure traveling through me. I run my fingers through his hair, wriggling with ticklishness as he kisses and kisses my skin everywhere he can. "That was...incredible."

"I pleased you well, then?" When I nod, he nips at my hip with his sharp fangs. "Good. I'd hate to think that the Pussy Patrol might walk away without, uh, satisfaction."

I tap his cheek. "You're not very good at the whole 'patrol' game, are you?"

He chuckles, his mouth against my skin so I feel his breath move ticklishly over me. "I'm better at other things."

I sigh, because he's not wrong. "You're definitely a man of action. I like that."

Sentorr continues to kiss my thighs and belly, as if he's content to be down there all day. "Tell me how long you need."

"How long I need?" His words aren't registering in my desire-addled mind.

"Before I can make you come again," he tells me, eyes still hot with arousal.

I realize I've pretty much been turned into a pile of happy, bone-less goo and he hasn't gotten to come at all. Nor have I had the chance to explore him like he has me. "I need a bit longer," I admit. I pat the blankets. "Why don't you come up here so I can touch you for a while?"

Sentorr groans and presses his face against my thigh. "I do not know if that's a good idea."

"Why not?"

"Because it might be too much for me. Even now, I ache for you so badly that..." He grits his teeth and shakes his head.

That he's on the edge? "We have all night," I cajole, sliding my hand over his blankets in another invitation. "And I want to learn your body. If you come all over my hands, then so be it. I just came all over your face, after all, and you didn't mind."

His teeth scrape over my thigh again, sending shivers through my body. "You can come on my face as many times as you want and I will always be greedy for more, Zoey."

"Exactly. So come up here and let me snuggle you for a bit." I run a teasing finger over the blankets. "It's something I've wanted for a long time."

When I pose it like he's doing me a favor, it seems to convince him. Reluctantly, he leaves his spot between my thighs and moves to sit next to me on the bed, and then pulls me into his arms and tucks me against his chest. I'm struck by how utterly devoted he is to my pleasure, and a little besotted, too. How did I get so lucky?

I put my hand on his chest, and I can feel his heart racing under my touch. He's plated and armored like all mesakkah, the thick, almost chitinous natural armor strangely sexy under my touch. I trace fingers along the ridges of one plate before sliding over to caress one rock-hard nipple. When Sentorr sucks in a breath and goes still, I slide out of his grip and sit on my knees, facing him. "Lean back so I can touch you."

His nostrils flare, lust evident in his eyes. "If you're sure."

"Don't make me call out the Dick Patrol," I tease, moving my hand to the waistband of his trou. They're made of a soft material, probably for sleeping, and his cock strains against the front, tenting the fabric. "I want to touch you and give you pleasure like you touched me. Is that so wrong?"

"I just don't want you to feel as if you have to—"

I snort. "After all the filthy late-night conversations we've shared, what part of this makes you think I'm feeling obligated?" I drag a finger along the outline of his cock, because it seems bigger than

I'd ever imagined. "I'm touching you because I've been dreaming about it forever."

Sentorr's jaw clenches, as if he's warring silently with himself. His gaze meets mine, and then he nods and retreats on the bed until his back is against the wall, his legs stretched out before him. It's not quite what I had in mind, but when he puts his hand on my face and caresses my arm, I realize he'd rather be sitting up so he can watch and touch me as I explore him.

Me likey.

I decide to start with kissing, because I'm addicted to kissing him. I put my hand on his cheek, turning his face so I can fit my mouth over his. He tastes hot and sultry at the same time, and I realize I'm tasting myself. I moan against his tongue, especially when his hand locks behind my head, pulling me against him so he can plunge into my mouth with deep, searing kisses that make the ache deep inside me even more pronounced. As he kisses me, I slide a leg over his thigh until I'm straddling him, just like I did back on the bridge. Except this time, I'm practically naked, and when I shrug off the tunic, I'm completely naked, parked atop him in nothing but a smile. His cock presses up against my pussy, and I feel the urge to rub up and down against his hot length. I want that more than anything, but I pause. He's mesakkah.

They are major fanatics about hygiene. "Uh, should we get some plas—"

"No," he tells me, and pulls me against him, until my breasts are against the heat of his chest and his mouth is on mine once more. I moan against his mouth, twining my arms around his neck even as he reaches between us and hits the fastener on his trou. In the next moment, he's pulling the clothes off and flinging them to the side, and then he's naked underneath me. Sentorr's hands slide to my ass and he drags me forward, settling me over his cock. "I want to feel you all over me."

And he rocks his hips.

I bite back another moan because the hard iron bar of his cock pushes through the folds of my pussy, teasing against my now ultra-sensitive clit. We could come like this, I realize. Because I know if he does I won't be far behind. I'm already incredibly turned on again, just by rubbing up against him and seeing the heat in his eyes. I love knowing that I do this to him. He's the sexiest male I've ever seen, and the fact that I'm here with him makes me feel like the luckiest girl in the universe.

"Kiss me," Sentorr demands. I want to protest that I'm supposed to be in control, that it's my turn to explore him, but I'm too fascinated by the possessive look in his eyes and the feel of his cock between my thighs. And I want to kiss him back.

I lean in and his mouth claims mine, his hand tangling in my hair. While he ravages my mouth with another deep kiss, his hand grips my ass, dragging me forward until I feel him fit his length not just against my folds, but sliding through them.

I gasp, because now I can feel everything.

He's impossibly huge, and I can feel the prod of his spur between us, but I'm too distracted to finish my exploration. I'm lost in his kiss, in the friction of my nipples as they rub against his chest. He drags me lightly up and down against him, and his cock slicks along my folds, the head butting up against my clit, the ridges along his length making stars explode behind my eyelids.

"I don't think this was a good idea," I warn him, a whimper in my voice.

"It's the best idea," he tells me, and nips at my lower lip with those sexy fangs of his. "You're going to come again, aren't you?"

When I give a jerky nod, the breath hisses from between his teeth. "I love how sensitive you are. You're perfect, Zoey. My perfect, sweet mate."

I whimper again when his mouth claims mine. He thrusts up against the cradle of my thighs, his length strumming through my folds and making me crazy with need.

"I'm not going to claim you tonight," he murmurs between kisses.

"You're not?" I gasp as he thrusts up against me once more. Oh god, those ridges on his cock are so unfair.

"No. I'm going to wait until you move in with me. After we're properly mated." And he pumps up against me again.

I dig my nails into the hard armor on his shoulders, barely aware of what he's saying. His hips and the slide of his now-slick cock are far too distracting. Something about me moving in with him. "Gonna be hard to navigate my brothers' ship if I'm here in your bed," I tell him, lost as he thrusts up against me again.

"Let them navigate their own ship," he whispers, and clasps my breast, teasing my nipple. "You're my mate, Zoey."

But...wait. "Wait, wait," I breathe, still dazed with passion but something doesn't seem right. "You want me to leave my brothers? Leave my post on the *Little Sister?*"

Sentorr gives me another hard kiss, one that makes my toes curl and my body sing. Between presses of his mouth to mine, he tells me, "I love you, Zoey. I want you to join me here. I'll make you happy."

Oh. Spending my days with him on the bridge and nights in his bed? The thought blooms in my chest with pleasure...and then quickly pops like a bubble. "I can't."

"What do you mean, you can't?" Sentorr's eyes, passion-glazed just a moment ago, grow narrow as they focus on me. "You're my mate and I'm yours. You belong with me."

I...never thought further ahead than the next flirtation with Sentorr. I never thought I'd meet him, so perhaps that's why I'm so utterly floored—and sickened—at the realization of what it means to be in love with him.

He wants me to be with him. I want to be with him.

But I owe Mathiras, Adiron and Kaspar my life. They took me in, raised me and treated me better than any human girl deserves to be treated by three grown mesakkah pirates. They could have sold me off for quick cash, and instead, they trained me to be a navigator and have always had my back.

I can't abandon them, no matter how much I want Sentorr. "You can join us on the *Sister*," I tell him. "We can navigate together."

He shakes his head, leaning in to kiss me again. "They need me here on the *Fool*. The others aren't trained to nav. They don't know the ins and outs like I do. Well, Kivian does, but I think Fran's pregnant. They're going to need more time together, not less. I can't leave."

I pull away before his lips can brush mine again. "They need you here. My brothers need me, too."

"I need you," Sentorr tells me, cupping my face in his hands. "Zoey, I love you."

But if I love him, I have to give up my family and my ship. Horrified at the thought, I pull out of his grasp. "What you want, I can't give you. I'm sorry." I slide off of his lap, scoop up my tunic, and race back to my room. It's amazing I manage to do it so quickly, but panic does wonders for speed.

Once the doors shut behind me, I sag against the wall and let the tears come.

I never thought what falling in love would mean for my brothers. I can't be selfish and cost them a navigator. I can't. I owe them my life. I owe them more than I can ever possibly imagine, and I'll always owe them. I can't sacrifice the happiness of three men who've been amazing to me just because I've lost my heart to a stern, too-proper former soldier who loves me despite the fact that I'm human.

I bury my face in my hands and weep.

11

SENTORR

*Z*oey avoids me all morning. She's not in the mess hall when I head in for breakfast, and when I go to her door and knock, she doesn't answer. Eventually I head to the bridge to lose myself in navigation charts and guiding the *Fool,* but even that feels different now. She's been such a part of why I enjoy spending time there that it feels like something's missing. It's impossible to concentrate, and the slow tick of hours passing makes me irritable. I snarl at anyone that comes by to speak to me, and even though Alyvos is supposed to be watching the bridge right now, I send him off to spend time with Iris.

If I can't talk to Zoey, I don't want company.

I want to stew.

So I prod at my charts, making minor course corrections to give myself something to do other than think about her hands on my cock, the wet slide of my shaft between her folds and the little gasping noises she made, the heavy sway of her beautiful breasts, the look in her eyes when she came. The way she felt. The way she tasted.

I want her in my life. I want all my nights like last night, with Zoey in my arms, her skin against mine.

I won't give her up, I decide. I just need to think of a plan to keep her with me, to convince her that I need her more than her brothers.

I'm so busy concentrating on and discarding different plans to make Zoey stay on the *Fool* that I don't notice she's entered the bridge until she's standing right next to my station. I turn, both pleased and surprised to see her. "Zoey, you—"

My mate rushes forward and kisses me, as impulsive and sweet as ever. I bite back a groan, returning the hot, hungry kiss with one of my own. Our mouths meld for a blissful interlude and then she breaks free, panting as she rests her smooth forehead against my rugged one.

"I've made a decision," she murmurs.

"What's that?" I try to keep the excitement out of my voice. She's come to her senses, then. She's realized that we're meant to be together.

Her fingers curl around my collar, pulling me close. "We find someone else to watch the bridge for now and head to your room. We kef like mad for the next few days and squeeze in as much together time as possible until my brothers return. Then, in a few months, when we both have a hole in our schedule again, we meet up once more and do it all over." And she smiles at me.

I pull away, a frown on my face. "You'd be happy to be apart for months on end?"

"Well, I wouldn't be happy about it, no, but it's the best compromise—"

"You're my mate. I'm yours. I don't want to compromise." I reach out and take her hand in mine. "I want you at my side."

"I want that too, Sentorr, but I can't abandon my brothers." Her eyes are pleading for me to understand.

"So you'll abandon me."

"No!"

"Zoey." I cup her lovely, fragile face in my hands. "I want you. I want you all the time. I love you. It would destroy me to only have fragments of your time and to know that you're out at the far ends of space and I might not see you for months on end. Or years. I know as well as you do that our ships head in very different directions much of the time. I can't claim you as mine and then watch you go. That's not something I can do."

"Sentorr, please." Her eyes fill with tears. "Take what I can give."

"I want all of you," I tell her simply. "If I can't have that, then I will wait until I can."

ZOEY

The next three days are the longest of my life.

It's obvious to everyone on the ship that something's gone wrong between me and Sentorr. The fun dates we were supposed to have are canceled. He spends all his time on the bridge, staring at his monitors while the ship runs on automated lanes. He's clearly not paying attention, but he also won't spend his time with me.

He says it's better if we don't get too attached.

Problem is, I'm already attached. I feel as if my heart is breaking every day. I see him on the bridge, distant and sad, and I want to kiss him and hold him.

He won't let me, though. He looks at me, expectant, and when I shake my head, the light dies in his eyes and he turns back to staring at his monitors.

The others are aware, I think, of the fact that we've had a falling out of sorts. Fran and Cat and Iris do their best to be good hostesses, talking about Earth and sharing their contraband snacks as if I remember any of them. It's been so long that my tastes are more mesakkah than human...but I appreciate that they're trying. Even the other guys on the crew seem to be nice, though Alyvos just scowls at me constantly, despite Iris's chiding hand-squeezes. It's obvious he feels I was playing with Sentorr's feelings.

Maybe I was. Maybe I still am.

I just never thought further ahead, of what would happen if we truly fell in love. I know I could be happy with him. I like the rest of the crew on the *Fool*. It's impossible not to—I don't even mind Alyvos's scowls, because he's just defending his buddy Sentorr, and I love Sentorr.

But my brothers need me. Kaspar's a shit navigator and would burn a fortune in fuel, because he doesn't think ahead. Adiron just doesn't think at all. Mathiras thinks too much. They need me for balance. I'm the one that tells Kaspar to cool his heels. I'm the one that Adiron picks on and teases because Mathiras will lose his shit if Adiron glues his boots shut again. And I'm the one Mathiras talks to late at night when he's full of worries and needs someone to unload on.

My brothers are three extremes and they need a moderating presence with them. Someone good with navigation and money that will rein in Kaspar when he gets one of his wild, reckless ideas. Someone that will endure Adiron's endless teasing and his dopey jokes and lack of ambition. Someone that will help Mathiras shoulder the burden of running a successful pirate crew because his other two brothers aren't good at responsibility.

They saved me ten years ago. I save them every single day.

But...they need me in a different way than Sentorr needs me. Crew-wise, he doesn't need me at all. The *Fool* has a nav. He's a good enough navigator, of course. He's a great one. But I think in different ways than he does, and I know if we worked together we could come up with exciting paths and fuel-efficient ideas, and ways to skate around heavily watched star-lanes of traffic. We'd be unstoppable. But he doesn't NEED me.

Not like that.

He needs me to hold him close at night. He needs me to kiss him. He's lonely. I can tell he's lonely. He's always been lonely, ever since he left his family behind on Homeworld and ended up stationed on a distant shithole of a planet with no one around to talk to. He's lonely like I am, where you're surrounded by people but you still feel isolated.

I understand him.

And I love touching him and kissing him. I think of spending every night in his arms and want to cry with how badly I want it.

But obligation and family come first. They have to.

THE NEXT DAY, I stand near the hatch, watching as the docking tube extends from the *Little Sister* over to the *Fool*. The others have said their goodbyes and wished me well, and now it's just me and a silent Sentorr waiting for the final connection to be established so I can cross over between ships.

I feel dead inside.

All these days we had together? Wasted. We could have spent them in bed, loving each other and soaking in every moment we have together. Instead, the hours were miserable and alone. He wants me desperately, but he won't kiss me or hold me or make love to me because I can't give him forever. The sad thing is that I want to give him forever, but it's not mine to give. I have a duty to my brothers.

There's a hiss as the docking tube connects, and then a flash of green lights. "That's my cue," I say, keeping my voice bright and a smile pinned to my face even though I'm screaming inside.

He grabs my wrist, and I turn toward him, hope in my eyes. *Say that you're coming with me,* I silently beg. *You be the one to abandon your crew.*

"Stay," he asks me, his voice ragged with emotion. "Zoey, stay with me. Let's not end it like this."

"You could come with me."

Sentorr hesitates, then shakes his head. "There's no one trained. I won't leave them without a navigator."

"Then we both have the same problem," I tell him lightly. "You can't leave your crew and I won't leave mine."

"I love you," he tells me fiercely, pulling me close and giving me a hot, hungry kiss that's full of all the need and longing tearing at us both. "Stay with me. Don't choose them over you and me."

I flinch, because everything in me wants to scream that he's wrong...but I know he's not. "I'm sorry," I tell him, and pull away.

He lets me go, his face empty of emotion. I tap the hatch release and then step into the docking tunnel...and glance back at him.

Sentorr watches me, stone-faced. My lip quivers and I raise a hand to wave goodbye.

My beautiful man extends his hand toward me, too, but not in a wave. He holds it out to me, a silent request for me to put my hand in his and rejoin him. To stay at his side.

It feels as if everything in me is breaking. I turn away and head blindly through the docking tube. I hear the hiss of the seal behind me, and then the *Little Sister's* hatch opens and Adiron is there, waiting for me. I fall into his arms, sobbing as the hatch slides shut once more.

I'm home. Sentorr's gone.

Adiron wraps his big arms around me and strokes my hair. "Hey, Zo. It's going to be okay. It is." When all I can do is cry, he hugs me tighter. "Do I need to go over there and kick his ass?"

And then I'm laughing and sobbing at the same time, because I'm pretty sure Sentorr with his military training could kick Adiron's ass...but I love that he'd still volunteer it for my sake.

It doesn't make things hurt less, but it helps all the same.

12

SENTORR

I try not to tap my fingers impatiently as the crew slowly gathers in the mess hall. Kivian asked for the meeting today and I'm the first one here—as I always am. Alyvos and Iris show up next and sit down at the far end of the table, holding hands. Alyvos watches his mate with such intense, quiet joy that I can't look at him. It reminds me what I've lost. Cat and Tarekh show up a minute after the meeting's due to start, her arms around his neck as she catches a ride on her mate's back, whispering in his ear and grinning as if they just rolled out of bed. Judging from Tarekh's satisfied expression, it's a safe bet.

Naturally Kivian's late to his own meeting, but that's Kivian for you.

I cross my arms and lean back in my chair. I'm restless and irritable. Normally I'd be itching to return to the bridge and my workstation, but lately it hasn't held the same appeal. There's no flirty Zoey message waiting for me to return, no audio comm to connect to and chat over. Since she left the *Fool* a week ago, I've sent her a message. One.

I'll be here waiting for you.

That's it. More would just be harassment. She knows how I feel. If she changes her mind, I'll welcome her with open arms and joy in my heart. It won't happen, though.

Not for the first time, I consider what it'd be like if I left the *Fool* and joined their crew. No one here's appropriately trained yet, though. Maybe in time...but for now, nav duties continue to fall solely on my shoulders.

"I can't believe Kivian's not here," Tarekh says, gently depositing Cat on a chair before sitting down on his own. His irrepressible mate immediately abandons her chair and sits in his lap, slinging her arm around his neck.

"Can't you?" Alyvos's voice is dry with sarcasm. "Because I can believe it."

"I'm sure he'll be along soon," Iris adds with a smile, a bright blue ribbon over her eye-scars today that matches her tunic. "We're not meeting over anything bad, I hope."

"Doubtful," Alyvos tells his mate, toying with a lock of her dark hair.

I remain silent, watching them interact and fighting the gnawing jealousy in my gut. Zoey should be here, in my lap and murmuring naughty things like Cat's doing to Tarekh. Or she should be at my side, leaning in to my caress like Alyvos and his Iris. I can guess what the meeting's about. I can also guess why Kivian and Fran are late. Things are changing on the *Fool* once again.

Everything's the same for me, though. I'm alone and it feels as if there's a hole in my chest because my mate's not here at my side.

The door opens and Kivian heads inside, wearing a plain tunic over his trou, which isn't like him. He looks slightly disheveled, but less so than Fran, who has a sickly cast to her golden skin and a faint sheen of sweat on her brow.

"Um, are you guys okay?" Cat asks.

Kivian helps Fran to a seat at the head of the table, guiding her with a firm arm around her waist. She gives him a grateful look as she sits and he retrieves a glass of water for her. "Kivian's fine," Fran says after a moment, her voice tired. She rubs her brow.

"I am most certainly not fine," Kivian retorts. "I don't like seeing you like this, love. Say the word and I'll steal a doctor."

"You're sick?" Iris asks, her face turning toward Fran's seat.

Tarekh just smirks, leans in to Cat and whispers something in her ear. Her eyes go wide, her jaw dropping.

I know exactly what ails her. After all, I'm the one that arranged her meeting with an ooli selling fertility enhancers three station visits ago. Looks like they took.

"I'm pregnant," Fran says. "It's just a bit of morning sickness."

"Morning sickness?" Kivian's horrified. "Not just morning, love. It's three in the afternoon. And you vomited all over my favorite tunic, the bed, my boots, and the lavatory. If this is morning sickness it needs to confine itself to morning alone. My clothes won't be able to take much more." But he leans in and strokes Fran's dark hair away from her brow. "Should we kidnap a doctor? I'm game."

Tarekh—our medic—clears his throat.

"Oh, kef off," Kivian tells him with a growl. "This is different."

"Because it's your mate?" he asks, amused.

"Precisely."

Fran just rolls her eyes. "We came here to tell you guys this, and to talk about living quarters."

Alyvos slides his arm protectively over the back of Iris's chair. "What about them?"

"Simply put, we need more of them. This ship has served us well for many years, but we're no longer a four-person crew. The way I look at it, we can have the *Fool* overhauled and more space added...or we can pool our funds and purchase a newer, bigger ship."

"Overhauled?" Fran asks. "How do you add rooms onto a ship?"

"Not easily," Tarekh says. "I'm not a fan of doing that. It destroys the structural integrity. Plus, with the engine we have, we're supposed to be lighter. We'd need a new darkmatter converter if we're going to pull more mass along, and those aren't cheap."

Kivian looks to me. "Sentorr?"

It's on the tip of my tongue to tell him that I don't care. That it doesn't matter to me if we're flying a junkerbus or the *Fool,* because I'm still a hollowed-out shell of a person without Zoey. But I try to look at things in a practical sense, to be part of the team. "The *Fool's* old," I admit. "She's served us well, but there are newer, sleeker models coming out every year. We could switch ships for a fraction of the cost of what it'd cost to rebuild her into something with more living space."

Zoey would like more living space, too, I think...if she were here.

"Alyvos?" Kivian asks.

"Don't care either way," he says, and then pauses. "But...I'd like Iris to have more room. Maybe enough space for a child of our own at some point."

Iris's cheeks flush and she smiles sweetly at her mate.

"Good." Kivian rubs his hands together. "It seems we're all on the same page, then. I've been talking to my brother Jutari and he knows someone with a Class II Homeworld warbird that they'd be willing to part with for the right price. It's off the records and everything, which is important for our business."

Tarekh's frowning. "That'd only work if it was refurbished with a skater-class engine to pull the speed we need."

Kivian just grins. "Funny you should mention that..."

13

ZOEY

Two Weeks Later

SOMETHING FLICKS against my hair as I sit at my station on the *Little Sister.* Star charts are spread on the screens before me, shipping lanes mapped and possible routes twisting through the nearest system are being traced by the algorithms in the computer to determine which one's going to be the best for fuel, speed, and secrecy. I should be paying attention. Instead, I'm staring blankly out the window at a distant colorful nebula and wondering where Sentorr is. If he misses me.

Because I sure keffing miss him.

My hair twitches again, and I reach out to brush it away from my face—only to encounter something cold and slimy. With a gasp of horror, I pull a blue noodle from my hair. What the kef...

Behind me, Adiron snickers.

I turn and fling the noodle across the bridge at him. "You are such an ass!"

He dodges my throw and plucks another from his bowl, slurping it up without using a utensil. "You gonna make me pay for it?" His tail flicks a challenge on the nearest wall.

I glare at him and turn back to my monitors. "No. Leave me alone."

This time, Adiron gives a gusting sigh. "You are no fun anymore, Zo."

"I'm sorry to disappoint you," I snap at him. "I'll try to be more entertaining." I find another piece of noodle on my shoulder and flick it away. "I had no idea that was part of the keffing job."

"It's not. I'm just wondering how long you're going to mope over this male."

Just thinking about Sentorr makes me want to cry again. "Until it stops hurting." My voice sounds wobbly, even to my own ears.

"Have you tried talking to him?" I shake my head and he continues on. "Don't you think you should? I bet he's miserable, too."

I turn and look over my shoulder at my big, beefy brother. Of all three of them, I'm closest to Adiron. He's a pain in the ass, but he's got a good heart under there, somewhere. "Are you giving me love advice? In the last ten years, have you even met a woman that's not a space hooker of some kind?"

He just grins at me. "I know how it feels to get your heart broken, that's all."

"I bet you do," I mutter, starting another calculation once one finishes. "Every time they ask you to pay for the keffing instead of giving you a freebie."

His laughter howls through the bridge. "Sentorr know you're so feisty?"

I shoot him the finger, an Earth gesture that's still incredibly appropriate.

He only laughs again, and it's clear that my prickliness is entertaining to him. "I'm just saying, you're only making yourself miserable. If you want this male, go and get him. We checked him out and he's acceptable, so you don't have to worry about that part."

Acceptable? I frown at my screens, tapping away to run the same query again just to keep my hands busy. "What are you talking about?"

"Mathiras had his buddy that's at the credit company run a scan on his financial records. They're flush, which is good. He can buy you a ship if he needs to. Kaspar pulled his identity through three different security databases and the last records they have of him is when he was in the military. No warrants for arrest, no sketchy past history, no mate back on Homeworld."

I slowly turn in my chair, glaring at Adiron. "I can't believe you did that. You guys were checking up on him?"

Adiron snorts and sets his bowl down on the nearest surface. "I can't believe you thought we'd leave you with him for a few days and not check that sort of thing first."

"I'm a big girl," I protest.

"You are, but you're also our little sister and we look out for you."

Hot tears blur my vision once more. He's wonderful. They all are...and that's precisely the problem. They're so caring and amazing that I can never leave them, even if I feel hollowed out inside from missing Sentorr. "Just...tell me this gets better. That this hurting goes away. That I'll forget about him at some point."

Adiron gets to his feet. He moves to my side and puts a hand on my shoulder in a comforting squeeze. "I can't tell you that. I can't tell you it gets better anytime soon, because I met a girl once and thought she was my mate. Turns out she was a liar and a cheat and already had a male. Lost my faith in all females after that. So no, I can't tell you it gets better. When we love, we love with all of our hearts and everything we are. But you know what I can tell you?"

I swipe at my eyes, sniffing. "What?"

"You've got a noodle in your ear." Before I can ask what he means, he shoves another cold, slimy noodle at me, ignoring my squeals of horror.

As pep talks go, it's not the best, but he's trying.

14

SENTORR

 y heart leaps in my chest when I see the hail from the *Little Sister*. It's early afternoon, which is unusual for Zoey, but I'm alone on the bridge anyhow. It was Kivian's turn to spell me, but I chased him off, telling him to spend time with Fran instead. It's not like I'm good company, and I find myself too restless to sleep these days. So I work. I chart sample flights on paths I've already gone down a thousand times before in the hopes of new information. I route and reroute the *Fool* a dozen times an hour.

And now, all the waiting's paid off. For three long weeks, I've hoped that Zoey would contact me and tell me she's changed her mind. That she can't bear to be apart from me either.

I answer the comm with joy leaping through my chest...only to feel it crash when Kaspar's blue face peers into the vid screen. He nods at the sight of me, and then elbows someone off-screen. "He picked up. Get in here, you two." With a tap, the vid widens and then I'm looking at all three of her brothers' faces.

Fear clenches my gut. Something bad has happened. "Zoey. What's wrong with her? Tell me where you're at and I'll be there immediately." It doesn't matter what the situation is, or that we're en route to Kivian's brother Jutari's backward planet to pick up our new warbird. Zoey needs me.

"Calm the kef down," Kaspar says. "We just need to talk to you."

"You look like shit," Mathiras adds.

"Baked shit," Adiron agrees. "I see it's not just Zoey. She misses you, you big dumb bastard. Why'd you let her go if she's your mate?"

I rub a hand over my brow. "Zoey's all right?"

"If by 'all right' you mean heartbroken and weepy and not herself? Yeah, she's keffing fine," Kaspar growls, leaning back and crossing his arms over his chest. "She barely sleeps anymore and she's like a ghost. All because things didn't work out with you. I want to know what you said to her."

They blame me? Instead of being offended, I'm touched. These three men really do care for their sister in the best way. She's lucky to have them. "I believe my exact words were 'don't go' and 'stay.'"

They look at each other. "Explain," Mathiras says.

"Zoey is perfect in every way. She has my heart and I let her know it. But she won't be with me because she feels she owes you her life. She feels she cannot abandon you. That you need her as a navigator and a sister and for her to seek her own happiness would be betrayal."

Mathiras frowns. Kaspar rubs his chin, thinking. Adiron just rolls his eyes.

"She's not happy," Mathiras finally says. "That's all we've ever wanted is for her to be happy. Doesn't have to be with us. We'll support her in whatever choice she makes."

"And Zoey thinks her choice has to be us." Kaspar rubs his chin again, thoughtful. "We need to give her back her choices, then."

I grip the edge of the control panel, trying to keep my eagerness hidden. Zoey. I'd give anything to see her again. "Tell me what you have in mind."

15

ZOEY

J stare at the tired woman in the mirror, wondering how long it takes for a broken heart to stop showing on my face. It's been a month since I saw Sentorr. A month with a shattered heart in my breast. A month since I decided to give up any hope for love. A month since I've heard Sentorr's smooth, liquid voice and had it send shivers up my spine.

It's been harder than I thought.

Silly me, I assumed that I'd return to the ship and everything would go back to normal. That I'd take up my duties and forget all about our in-person flirtation. Except...I can't. I can't concentrate because I can't stop thinking about Sentorr and his kiss. The way it felt when he touched my face. His mouth, his smile, the way he holds himself so very erect as if he's got a ruler strapped to his back. Even that I find sexy.

And now that I've experienced a taste of what it'd be like to be loved, I can't go back to the way I was. I can't forget him. I can't forget how it felt to be kissed, to be caressed, to be held in his arms. I can't forget how it felt to be LOVED. I turned my back on that and it feels as if there's this big aching hole in my chest and I'm just walking around wounded all day. When I close my eyes at night, I think of all the things I could have said to him, the ways I could have touched him.

He was my chance at love. I don't want anyone but him.

I feel so much regret that I had to choose the way I did. I love my brothers, but it's a different kind of love than what Sentorr can give me, and it's not enough.

How stupid am I that I thought it would be?

Before I met him, all I wanted was that flirtation. That sweetness to look forward to during long, quiet nights. The company. The affection.

I don't have any of it now. Sentorr's gone quiet and I can't contact him, because I know if I do, he'll ask me to return to him. I want to desperately, but I can't. So I hide my feelings, hoping that they'll fade in time, and I go through the motions. At least, I try to. I'm not sleeping, though. Every time I lie down I think of Sentorr. Is he as sad as I am? As miserable? Or has he already forgotten me? Is he finding some pretty mesakkah hooker on a station to ease his troubles? I doubt it, but my mind likes to have me imagine the worst. I would want him to be happy if I couldn't be with him, right? Theoretically I should, but the thought of him being with someone else makes me want to scratch their eyes out.

Which just makes me feel worse.

I splash water on my face and give one last hearty glare at my reflection before toweling off and heading out of my quarters. I tug my hair back into its regular ponytail and yawn as I head to the bridge. I need some night tea to get me through another evening without Sentorr. Night tea and a whole lot of tissue.

Of course, when I get on the bridge, I forget all about tea or anything else, because there's a massive warbird directly in the line of sight of the windows, and we're heading right for it. I make an outraged sound and race to my station, where Kaspar's napping, his head pillowed on the control panels. "What the kef are you doing?"

He lifts his head, blinks, and then rubs his eyes. "Napping?"

"We're on a collision course for that ship, you idiot," I snap, pushing him out of my chair and pulling up screen after screen. We're not off course, which means that this was planned. I glare at Kaspar again for being so careless as I begin to reroute the thrusters and pull up information on the ship in our sights.

Homeworld Class II warbird, now privately owned, my screen reads. The *Jabberwock*.

Kaspar peers over my shoulder. "What's a jabberwock?"

"It's a human thing," I snap at him. "Did you intend for us to hurtle right towards them? Or are you just that careless?"

He scratches his head and then grins at me. "...Yes?"

I make another outraged sound, slap my earpiece into my ear and then send an audio comm request to their navigator. "You'd better hope I can fix this! As it is, we're going to be scraping their hull in about five minutes flat."

"Huh," is all he says, and makes me want to choke him.

Keffing idiot. This is why I can't leave them. This—

The *Jabberwock* connects to my comm request. "Hail, *Little Sister*," says a smooth, familiar voice that makes my knees weak. If I wasn't sitting down, I'd be collapsing. As it is, I feel dreadfully close to falling to the floor in a boneless puddle.

"Sentorr?" I whisper. "What...?"

I turn to look at Kaspar. He's got his arms crossed over his chest and he's just grinning. As I stare, he reaches over me and overrides the reroute on my screen. "Prepare to launch the docking tube for cross-ship meeting."

Cross-ship meeting? I just stare dumbly as the *Jabberwock* accepts the request, and we smoothly pull up alongside the warbird. "I... don't understand," I finally manage.

"We need to resolve this with a face-to-face meet, Zoey. Permission to come aboard?"

"Um, granted," I say weakly.

"See you soon," Sentorr tells me and then disconnects.

I whirl about in my chair, giving Kaspar an accusing look. "What the kef is going on?"

"Weren't you listening? Ship-to-ship meeting," he says, whistling to himself as he saunters away. "You should probably hurry. Tube's gonna be connected in no time."

I manage another choked sound before I race out of my chair and head to my quarters. Oh my god. I'm wearing a stained standard-issue jumper. I furtively smell the armpit as I plunge into my room, then dig around in my laundry for something fresh. Kef. Kef. Kef. Why didn't I wash my hair today? I touch it and it feels frizzy and tousled, and I dash toward the lavatory instead, abandoning all thought of changing clothes when nothing leaps into my hands. I moan at my reflection, because I have circles under my eyes and I'm so, so pale. My hair's a mess.

To think that Zoey of a month ago didn't want to wear makeup or fix her hair to please a man. That Zoey was obviously full of lies. I smooth my fingers over my face, then wet them in the sink and try to pat down the worst of my flyaways in my hair. Sexy, I'm not. I look like any other unwashed, overtired navigator on a flight mission to the Outer Rim...which is what I am.

But this is different.

This is my man coming to see me again. I need to be so stinking pretty that he'll be overcome with passion and sweep me off my feet. Of course, that's probably not Sentorr, I think wryly to myself. He's more the type to stare down at me coldly and then demand that I kiss him.

Which is still freaking hot.

Nervous, I try to fix my hair one last time. The docking chime sounds overhead and I race back out of my room and down the winding halls of the *Little Sister,* toward the ship-to-ship hatch.

I lurch forward, past my brothers who are lined up in the narrow hallway, just as the hatch opens and Sentorr steps inside. He's larger than life, taller than I remembered, and so gorgeous and proud that I croak like a frog at the sight of him. Somewhere behind me, Adiron snickers. I don't care. He's here. My Sentorr's come back. I stand in front of him like an adoring idiot, hungrily devouring the sight of him. As he steps forward, though, it occurs to me that he's on the wrong ship.

Oh no.

Oh no, maybe this isn't a good thing after all. "What happened to the *Fool?*" I blurt out, suddenly terrified. Has his crew been killed? Are they being hunted? "Do we need to hide you? Or—"

Firm hands grasp my upper arms and Sentorr shakes his head at me. "Calm yourself. Everyone's well. No one's being hunted." He pauses. "At least not on this end of the galaxy."

"Where's your ship? Why are you here? How did you—"

"Let the man speak, Zo. Kef me." Adiron nudges my shoulder. "You're freaking out on him."

Am I? I am. I blink rapidly, full of emotions. "Sorry."

"Actually, I didn't come here to speak," Sentorr says, looking down at me. "I came to do this." His tail curls around my waist, locking around me, and then he pulls me close and his mouth descends on mine. His kiss is scorchingly hot, full of promise and need and lust and all of the good, yummy things I've been longing for in the last month, all the things I thought I'd never get. I whimper against him, my hands curling in the front of his uniform and I don't know who's clinging to who, just that we're locked together and I never want to let go.

Adiron makes a gagging sound somewhere behind us.

"That's my sister's face you're sucking," Kaspar says. "Can you not?"

Sentorr gives my mouth a sensual lick before releasing me. He grins at the dazed expression on my face and cups my cheek. "I want you to come back with me to the *Jabberwock*. Or I'll come here to the *Sister*. Either way, I want to be with you."

I sag against him, all happily boneless as I gaze at his mouth. It's still damp from our kisses and I want to taste it again. In fact, I barely register what he's saying, and then it sinks in. "Wait... *Jabberwock*? What happened to the *Fool*?"

"Quarters were getting tight," he tells me, running his thumb along my lower lip as if he's unable to stop touching me. "Kivian knew someone that was selling a warbird off the records, so we took it off his hands."

Mathiras whistles. "A warbird. Fast and dangerous—best of both worlds."

My gorgeous man grins. "Luckily I piloted one back when I was in the military, so it's a lot like coming home for me."

"Oh," I breathe. I've always lusted after warbirds. Well, and Sentorr. The thought of running nav on one of them is tempting, but I know my brothers can't spare me. "Your crew has another navigator?"

"Not exactly." He shakes his head. "I'm choosing you over them."

I make a small sound of protest in my throat, because...warbird. And his crew is so nice. I'd love to hang out on a ship like that. It seems wrong for him to abandon them, especially when navigation's one of the most important—if not the most—jobs on the ship itself.

Mathiras clears his throat. "I think you should go with them, Zo."

I turn to look at my brother in surprise. "You do?"

He nods. "We all do."

Kaspar winks at me. Adiron just grins.

I realize I've been set up. Kaspar didn't kef up the navigation. He arranged to meet Sentorr so they could transfer me over. Hurt stabs through me. I pull away from Sentorr's arms, torn. "You're getting rid of me?"

"No," Mathiras says. He moves to my side and puts his hands on my shoulders. "We love you. When we say you're our little sister, we mean it. Kef, we're closer to you than we are to our blood sister, Vanora."

I smile, but my eyes are filling with tears. If we're so close, why are they getting rid of me?

"But you need to be happy. It's clear that you're in love with this stiff-necked soldier." Mathiras nods at Sentorr. "And he's needed on his ship. And you need him. Which is why you need to go."

"Plus, there's other humans on board," Kaspar says. "Human females. It'll be good for you to be around others of your kind. They can support you in ways we can't."

"Like hair braiding," Adiron says, and makes a kissy face. "And helping each other dress."

"Kef me, if they're helping each other dress, I want to go watch," Kaspar mutters.

Mathiras turns and glares at both of them.

I don't point out how right Kaspar is, or that they've braided my hair in the past. "I wouldn't choose other humans over you guys. You know that!"

"Zoey," Mathiras says gently, squeezing my shoulders. "Just because you go with them doesn't mean you're abandoning us."

"Doesn't it?" I whisper, feeling as if my heart is breaking. A hand brushes mine and Sentorr locks his fingers quietly with my own in a silent show of support.

"You're our sister. That doesn't change if you're on this ship or another one. If you go with them, we'll cover nav until we get someone on full time. We've done it before. We can do it again."

"You'll burn too much fuel," I warn.

"We'll send him the bill," Adiron says. "He's loaded."

Sentorr only snorts and gives my hand a squeeze.

"But I won't get to see you guys," I whisper, looking up at Mathiras. I'm torn. So torn.

"We'll talk on the comm daily," he promises.

"And you can keep sending us charts and your star maps until we get someone new," Kaspar adds. "You'll just be sending them from afar."

Adiron's been pretty quiet (well, for Adiron), but he speaks up. "And we'll schedule visits with each other. Sentorr agreed to drag you out to visit us at least every other month. It'll be good for our ships to connect anyhow. We can network and share leads."

"Downtime will be good for all of us," Sentorr says quietly. "Especially with Fran and Kivian expecting a child."

Oh.

Oh...they're encouraging me to go. I look at my brothers' faces and it's clear that their biggest worry is my happiness. Nothing else matters. I burst into tears, flinging my arms around Mathiras's waist. "I love you guys."

"We love you, too, little sister," My oldest brother says, squeezing me tight then releasing me so I can hug Kaspar. He grabs me and hauls me against him, lifting my feet off the ground in a big bear hug that nearly empties my lungs, but then he puts me down again just as quickly—and just in time for Adiron to sling an arm around my neck and haul me against him, noogie-ing my hair.

"You'd better not forget us," Adiron tells me.

"Never." And I burst into tears again, because I'm going to go with Sentorr and leave my brothers behind and I'm so happy and so sad all at once.

"You don't have to go," Sentorr speaks up, and Adiron's hand on my head slows its painful drag. I slide out from under his grip and turn to face Sentorr. My beautiful, proud, stoic Sentorr with a soldier's bearing and a firm mouth that smiles only for me. He's not smiling right now. In fact, he looks almost pained. "The last thing I want is for you to be unhappy, Zoey. If you want to stay with them—

I fling myself into his arms and kiss him before he can say anything else.

I want this.

I want him.

16

SENTORR

Several hours later, the *Jabberwock's* engines purr as she glides out into deep space, away from the *Little Sister* and towards her next destination. Zoey's at my side, her bags on the end of my bed, and she sobs into my shoulder, curled up in my arms.

"I've never been away from them before," she tells me between fits of weeping. "W-what if they b-burn all the fuel and end up going broke?"

"They're pirates, Zoey. Corsairs. Being sly is what they do. If they burn all their fuel, they'll send out a distress beacon and rob whoever comes to bail them out."

She sniffles as I stroke her hair. "Just like those dicks on the asteroid did to us."

"That's right."

"I'm going to need to send Kaspar charts later tonight. And probably send him a program to let me course correct him from afar. He's keffing terrible at navigation, even if he thinks he's not." She rubs her wet face against my uniform, but I don't mind. It's already soaked with her tears.

"That's fine," I tell her. "We'll let Alyvos and Iris know we'll switch out with them later tonight."

She sits up and gives me a wobbly smile. "I'm sorry. I'm being a big baby, I know. Part of me knows they'll be fine. That they're probably heading to the nearest station so Adiron can stick his dick into some space hookers without his sister giving him shit over it, but part of me just worries."

I rub a hand down her back. I'm trying not to think about mating, because Zoey is sad and vulnerable right now, but it's hard not to. Not when she's curled up against me, her breasts pressing against my chest, her legs slung over my thigh. It's hard to think about anything but kissing her, tasting her all over.

But I don't want to push her, either. I've waited this long to have her, I can wait a few days more. "Of course you're going to worry," I tell her. "We'll check on them constantly, I promise. You think they won't be checking up on you? Making sure that I'm treating you right?"

That brings a smile to her watery eyes. "They probably bugged my gear so they could spy on us."

I smile back at her, but at the same time, I make a mental note to check her gear. Just in case. Because they ARE pirates. "And if you're ever not happy, I'll take you back to them in a heartbeat, no questions asked." It'll kill me, but I can endure just about anything but her tears. Those are tearing me apart.

Her fingers move along the front of my uniform, teasing the

fastening at the neck. "No. I'm happy. I missed you so much that I thought I would die with how badly it hurt, Sentorr. I kept thinking I'd made a mistake, but I didn't see how to fix it. I wanted you. I never stopped wanting you."

I rub my knuckles along her jaw, caressing her soft skin. "You've always had me. I was waiting for you. I'll keep waiting for you if I have to."

Zoey shakes her head. "You know what would make me feel better?" When her gaze meets mine, she says, "A nice, toe-curling orgasm."

I groan. "Zoey, there's no rush—"

"Good. That means I get to explore you this time. I didn't really get a chance last time. Is it true that your spur's sensitive on the underside? Is it hard to the touch? Can I touch it?"

She's going to kill me.

"Sentorr?"

I have no words, just hungry need. With an unsteady hand, I reach for my collar and undo the fastening there, then let the auto-seal slowly glide down. My Zoey makes an impatient noise in her throat and pulls at my clothing before the auto-seal can even finish opening my uniform, slipping her hand inside and caressing my chest. "I should have never touched you," she tells me, voice low and sweet even as her fingers graze over my nipple. "Because I didn't know what I was missing. When I did, it made losing you unbearable."

"You haven't lost me," I tell her, tugging her even closer against me. She's still curled up against my side, and I press a kiss to her hornless brow. Did I think humans were odd with their smooth, rounded heads? I like the feel of her like this against me, knowing she can't jab my face with one of her horns. She's perfect—dainty but fierce, delicate but fearless. I would change nothing about her.

"I'm so glad," she says, and then she pushes at my uniform, and I help her pull the sleeves off my arms. She admires my biceps, squeezing the hard muscle of one before tracing her fingers along the protective plating. Her expression is intense as she touches me, moving along my shoulder before heading down my chest and teasing my navel. Then, she moves to my trou, and a wicked little smile curves her pink mouth before she touches the fastener and it begins to undo.

I can't watch her staring at me with that ravenous expression. If I do, I'll come in my trou and the evening will be over. I kick off my boots and lift my hips as she tugs my trou down my thighs, trying to focus on anything but her so I can pace myself. "The, ah, new ship's quarters are bigger."

"So big," she purrs with agreement, and I can feel my cock jump as if she's talking about it and not the warbird.

"We have room on the bridge for six stations instead of four, and there's two extra crew rooms. Bigger rec area. Bigger mess hall. Bigger guns."

"Oh, I like big guns," Zoey says dreamily, and her hands move to the insides of my thighs, lightly caressing. She kneels at the edge of the bed, her breasts pressing against my bare legs.

I close my eyes, because this is the sweetest torture ever. "Two guest chambers, too. More than enough room for your brothers to visit."

"Mmm."

"If you want your own chamber, there's room for that, too." I know the human mates of the others in the crew sleep beside their males, but I don't want to push Zoey into anything too quickly. I can wait until she's ready.

"I want to be here with you," she tells me, and then her hands clasp my shaft. "You're so big."

I groan, forgetting all about rooms or warbirds. Nothing matters except Zoey's touch. "You like it?"

"God, yes." Her fingers trail down my length, grazing over heated skin. "Look at all these ridges." I can feel her shiver, her fingers gliding and caressing me. "That's definitely not a human thing."

"Have you seen a lot of human cocks?" I'm panting, trying to keep control.

"I watched some porn vids," she admits. "I wanted to know what it was like. They...weren't very sexy. But it was a good anatomy lesson. I like this better, though." She drags a fingertip over my sac. "You're bigger and prettier."

A laugh huffs out of me. "I don't know that most males want their cocks to be called pretty."

"But it is!" She grins at me and then moves her hands over me again. "You have a big, thick head here." And she traces a fingertip around the crown, sending crashing waves of lust through my body. "And you're a gorgeous, deep shade of blue. And there's a big vein along the top nestled in all these perfect ridges. And you're big, too." Zoey grips me with a light squeeze, as if testing my width. "I wasn't sure how big would be a good size, but I like this one. And...you have a spur."

And she lightly touches the tip of it.

I grit my teeth. I don't know which is the more pleasurable torture—her words, her touches, or the fascination on her face as she caresses me. My spur isn't as sensitive as the rest of my cock, so when she gives me an eager look after touching it, I nod at her. "You can touch it."

Her brows furrow. "I guess it's not like a clit where I practically jump off the bed if you touch mine."

I want to tell her that my cock's far more sensitive, but I also want her to do as she likes. If she wants to caress my spur for hours, I'll sit here quietly and let her explore to her heart's content. Any touch of her hands feels good. "I still like it."

"Yes, but I want you to go wild on me," Zoey says with a mischievous little grin. She strokes my spur with her thumb, caressing the underside and at the base, and I suck in a breath, because that felt...different. "Now we're getting somewhere," she tells me. "And I'm going to put my mouth on you. Do you want me to use plas-film?"

The hygienic, body-protecting film? "Only if you want to."

Her nose wrinkles adorably. "Me? No. You're the one from Home-world. They're all freaks about disease."

I laugh, though it comes out roughly because she's still caressing the underside of my spur and I'm about two seconds away from grabbing her by the hair and pushing her down on the mattress to kef the daylights out of her. Her touch is sending jolts through my body, and my cock feels harder by the moment. Pre-cum's beading on the head and Zoey notices it, too. She gasps and then looks up at me. "If we're not using plas-film...I'm going to taste you."

I bite back a groan. "Taste me, then," I tell her, voice ragged. I move a hand to her hair and caress her, though it's taking everything I have not to fist her locks and drag her down against me in the most primal of urges.

She gives me a mischievous look and then leans in, licking up a bead of pre-cum. The sight of her pink tongue flicking against my cock? The light stroke of it? I nearly come right then and there. I can feel the sweat break out on my forehead as she smiles at me. "I like it."

"Do you?" The words barely manage to rasp from my throat.

"Mmmhmm." She clasps her fingers around my cock and licks the head again.

I fall back onto the bed, lost. I always knew Zoey was a bit of a tease, but this goes beyond anything I have ever imagined. Nothing has ever felt better. I growl low in my throat, my hand fisting in her soft, soft hair as I do my best not to push her face forward, to guide her. I want her to have the freedom to use her mouth as she likes. And she does, licking her way up and down my shaft, tracing each ridge with the tip of her tongue and making little sounds as she does. After an agonizing length of time, she returns to the head of my cock, swirling her tongue over it, and then sucks me deep.

I suck in a breath, my sac tight against my body. I can feel my seed surging, my body ready to come, to pump deep into her. I'm so close to the edge that I gently pull her off of me. "Zoey," I pant. "Enough for now."

She looks up at me and thrusts her lower lip out, pink and shiny. "I'm not done."

"I will be if you keep touching me," I warn her and sit up. I pull her into my arms and claim her sexy mouth with mine, devouring her with one kiss after another. Zoey moans as I do, her leg sliding over me until she's straddling me once more. It feels amazing...but I need to make sure that she's hot and wet so when I ease into her, she won't feel any pain for her first time mating. I continue kissing and nibbling on that perfect, lovely mouth of hers and gently lower her to the blankets, dragging one leg up against my hip as I lie her beneath me. "My turn to touch you."

Her eyes flare with eagerness and she touches the fasteners on her clothing, helping me undress her. I don't take my time; I tear the fabric away from her body the moment it loosens, revealing her pale skin and soft curves. She gasps as I rip her clothing off, her body quivering, but her excitement is palpable. "Sentorr," she breathes, her hands going to my horns as I lower my mouth to her bare cunt.

I give her folds a long, hard drag of my tongue and she cries out, clutching at my horns as her hips rock and she pushes her thighs further apart, welcoming me between them. She's wet, aroused from touching me, but I want to make her soaking with need. I work her cunt with my tongue, tasting each fold and nuzzling it before gently sliding them apart and focusing my attention on the tiny bud of her clit.

Zoey cries out, arching up against my mouth and rubbing, as if she's desperate for the friction. I anchor one arm around her hip, pinning her as I work her cunt with my lips and tongue. She writhes against me, her honey slick and coating my mouth with her flavor, but she's small and human, and I am big and mesakkah. I have to make sure that she can take my cock.

Carefully, I push one finger into her core, even as I continue to work her clit with my tongue, alternately sucking and licking. She makes pleading noises as I slowly ease my finger into her tight channel. She's small, for all that she's hot and incredibly wet. I pump into her with gentle motions, until I'm able to add a second finger to her heat and use both to fill her like I want to with my cock. Her hips arch higher, and she clings to me, babbling insensible things as I lick her clit in steady motions, using both fingers and tongue to pleasure her.

Then she's keening her release, a fresh wave of sweet honey washing over my tongue as she comes. I continue to thrust into her, wringing every bit of pleasure out of her orgasm that I can, loving the way she holds on to me as she shudders with pleasure. It's as if I'm the only thing she trusts to hold her up when the world's crashing down around her, and it fills me with intense joy, even as it makes me hungrier than ever to claim her. My cock throbs and aches with need, and I grind against the blankets as I lap up her release.

She lets out a sultry little sigh, twitching every time my tongue moves against her clit. "Mmm, Sentorr, your tongue."

"You like it?" I slick it against her clit again, teasing.

A little moan escapes her. "Kef, yes."

I press a kiss to the inside of her thigh, then kiss my way up her belly. How did mesakkah males go entire lifetimes without putting their mouths on their mates? It's unthinkable. I can't imagine going a day without using mine on Zoey. I want to taste her everywhere—from her delicate toes to the curved shell of her ear.

But right now? I just want to sink deep into her.

I ply my mate with kisses as I move over her, dragging her leg up against my hip and resting my cock in the cradle between her thighs. She whimpers into my mouth, locking her legs around me and holding on to my neck. She's beautiful under me, and I thrust my cock through the wet heat of her folds, slicking it with her juices. As I do, she gasps, her breasts bouncing with the movement, and she's so lovely and it feels so good that I do just that for several long moments, stroking along her cunt, rubbing my cock in her honey and watching her plush breasts move as her body does.

Zoey reaches up and cups my cheek. "You know I love you, right?"

I groan. "I do. You have my heart as well." I take her hand in mine and press it over the plating on my chest, directly over my own heart.

She smiles shyly. "So you won't get mad if I tell you that I think you're doing it wrong?"

Doing it wrong...? I stare down at her.

"Penis goes inside," she whispers helpfully, and gives me a little nod. "I watched several vids about that."

I bark with laughter, my shoulders shaking. She...thinks I don't know how to mate her? "My gorgeous Zoey," I murmur, leaning in and pressing kisses on her face. "Your helpfulness knows no bounds."

"Not that what you're doing doesn't feel good," she says quickly. "It feels great, but I want you inside me."

Kef me, I want to be inside her, too. All of my humor vanishes, replaced with hunger. I cup her jaw, holding her mouth open as I lick her, and loving the way she goes from playful to needy within a heartbeat. She moans my name, and I nip at her lip. "You want what I can give you?"

Zoey shivers. "I do. Don't make me beg."

"Another time," I tell her. "We will play those games after I have claimed you thoroughly." I move a hand between us, adjusting our bodies until my cock fits at the entrance to her core. She moans, shifting against me, and I begin to press forward. Immediately, I realize just how tight she is, and I lean in to kiss her hard, capturing her mouth and taking it with deep, sensual kisses to distract her from the invasion of my cock.

The feel of her is exquisite, though. I want to lose myself in the sheer pleasure, but I can't.

Zoey feels differently, it is clear. Her cunt clasps me in a squeezing grip, and I kiss away her little whimpers of distress. "I won't hurt you, love. Relax. I have you."

She nods, trusting me, and lifts a finger to my mouth.

I nip at it, and she shivers again. "God, you're sexy."

"My heart," I tell her and kiss her again. Little by little, her body takes me deeper, and I flex my hips with controlled, careful movements, easing into her. It seems an impossible length of time, and I'm sweating with how badly I need her, but I don't want her to feel pain. I want this to be as good, as amazing for her as it is for me. So I kiss her, and kiss her, and work my cock in little strokes.

Eventually, the tension in her body eases and she meets my kisses hungrily. When I pump into her, she gasps, and then lifts her own hips to meet mine.

"Tell me how you feel," I demand, brushing a stray lock of hair from her lovely face. "Do you hurt?"

"It feels different than I thought," she admits. "You feel...so deep. I just...I can't describe it." And she hides her face against my neck.

"Do you want me to stop?" I think I might die if I pulled out of her now, but if she asks me to, I will. I slide my hand down her shoulder, touching her body and caressing one taut nipple in silent encouragement.

Her cunt tightens around my cock and she sucks in a breath. "No," she whispers. "Feels good." Zoey reaches between us and her fingertips graze my spur. "You know where that's hitting me?"

"The nub in your folds?" I ask.

She moans and nods. "Oh yeah. That's...gonna be wild."

"Want to try it now?" I circle my hips, moving in my first full stroke. My impatience is getting the better of me. I should wait longer, let her set the pace, but I need her so badly that I feel as if I might shatter if I don't claim her soon.

Zoey closes her eyes, sucking in a breath. The sound she makes is strangled, but when I try to pull off of her, she digs her nails into my shoulders. "Don't leave. Do that again."

A surprised laugh rumbles out of me. "My pleasure." I pull back and then stroke deep, claiming my mate the way I've dreamed for so long.

She gives a choked cry, her eyes closing. "Oh, kef me. I don't know what feels better—the ridges or the spur."

"Shall we try again and give you another chance to decide?" Without waiting for an answer, I pump into her again, flexing my hips. My tail flicks hard against the bedsheets, and when her legs clench tight around me, I wrap it around one ankle, anchoring her against me. "Better?"

Zoey just moans, her little nipples tight as they rub against my chest.

She's so keffing beautiful. "My mate," I growl low in my throat. "My Zoey."

"My god," she whispers as I thrust deep again. "Oh my god."

"Hold on to me." I kiss her once more, then begin a slow, steady motion. "Just hold on." I rock into my mate in steady, even thrusts, trying to establish a rhythm that will be as pleasing for her as it is for me. It's difficult, though, because with every thrust I make, she cries out and her body quivers around me as if she's on the verge of coming all over again. It makes every muscle in my body tighten in response, and my movements get jerkier, wilder, until I'm thrusting into her with all my might and she's crying out my name, our bodies rocking together with noisy slaps of flesh that make me feel as if I'm about to lose control. I need her to come first, though.

Nothing matters but her pleasure.

"Sen...torr," she pants between strokes. "I can't...I can't...need..." She makes a noise of frustration.

Needs more? More what? I palm her breast, rubbing the nipple, and she arches against me even as I pound into her. It's not enough, though, and I feel my own desire starting to overwhelm me. No.

Have to wait for her to come.

With a growl, I reach between us, searching for the spot where my spur shuttles against her clit, teasing her sensitive flesh. Zoey breathes my name again, and on a hunch, I reach down and squeeze her cunt tight, so when I stroke forward again, my spur touches her everywhere.

She breaks with a cry, and then her cunt is clenching and rippling around me, over and over, and my climax rips through my body. I plunge into her as I fill her body with my seed, claiming her as mine once and for all. Her tight channel is wet with my release, but I still rock into her, my movements slowing until they're mere twitches of my hips as I lie, panting, on top of her.

And yet I can't find it in myself to stop moving.

She gives a gusty sigh, her hands moving over my shoulders, and I press small kisses to her face. Even though I'm sated, I'm not ready to let go of her yet. I like being here over her far too much. I like seeing the flush in her cheeks, the sweaty tendrils of hair at her brow, the way her pupils are dilated with pleasure. Zoey reaches up and caresses my jaw, smiling sweetly at me.

"I'm an idiot," she says.

I press a kiss to her palm, chuckling. "Not what I expected to hear after claiming my mate. Why are you an idiot, my heart?"

Zoey smiles. "Because I didn't realize what I was missing out on when I chose to stay with my brothers. Now I could kick myself, because we could have had a month more of *that*."

Was ever a female so flattering to her male's ego? I can't help but grin. "You're loyal to your family. There's nothing wrong with that."

She slides her arms around my neck and pulls me down against her, snuggling against my neck. "Thank you for understanding." She inhales deeply. "Even your sweat smells good. I'm such a goner."

Fierce joy pounds in my chest, beating in time with my heart. "You are mine and I'm yours. Nothing else matters."

"Yes."

"Any regrets?" I can't help but ask.

"A month lost," she says again, and when I roll off of her, she makes a sound of protest. "We're done?"

"Well...you probably don't want me crushing you."

"Don't tell me what I want," she says impishly, pinching the tip of my tail as it flicks lightly over her body.

That sends a shudder through me that I feel right down to my cock. Minx. "Okay then, what do you want?"

"I want..." Zoey tilts her head and then teases my nipple with a fingertip. "I want to see where I'm going to sit."

"Where you're going to sit?" I echo, still dazed from our mating. Her nipples are taunting little buds dangerously close to my mouth still.

"On the bridge, silly." She flicks her finger over my nipple, tickling it and making my sac tighten in response. "I'm going to be navigating two ships now, you know. I'll need a prime seat. Near yours, preferably."

I laugh, because I love her eagerness. "You want to look now?"

"Well," she drawls, and thinks for a moment. "I mean, this *is* a warbird. But I can be convinced to stay in bed." Her eyes gleam with enthusiasm.

"Can you, now?"

"Oh, absolutely."

I smooth a hand down her belly. "Is this a shameless ploy to have me lick your cunt again?"

Her breath catches, and her eyes go dark with need. "Oh god, yes. Is it working?"

"Yes, yes, it is." And I grin at my mate and press a kiss to her belly.

"I'm all...we're both messy," she admits, a shy flush on her cheeks as she touches me.

"Not for long," I tell her, and I'm pleased with her low moan of response.

My beautiful, eager, filthy little mate. How I love her.

EPILOGUE

SENTORR

"*T*hey're here!" With glee, my mate flings herself out of her seat on the bridge and races toward the berth of the ship, where the ramp has been lowered. I follow behind a few steps, not racing myself, but also not willing to let Zoey go anywhere on Haal Ui Station without me nearby.

I get there just in time to see Zoey launch herself off the ramp and into the arms of Mathiras, who hugs her close, swinging her around. The moment he sets her down, Adiron grabs her, and I know Kaspar's just waiting his turn for his hug.

You'd think they haven't seen each other in a year. It's been more like two weeks. But I don't mind, because once they're all done hugging, Zoey launches herself back toward me, grinning. "Come say hi."

"I'm staying out of Adiron's grip," I warn all of them as I

approach. "No 'noogies' for me, thank you." I learned that lesson last time.

Adiron just smirks.

"You been taking care of our little sister?" Kaspar asks.

Zoey heaves an enormous sigh. "Oh my god, yes. He treats me great. Always makes me come at least twice before he nuts. Satisfied?"

I rub a hand down my face, reminding myself that she's a female raised by three foul-mouthed males. Of course she's going to say the same shocking things they do. It doesn't change how much I adore her, and when I growl low in my throat, she only winks at me and gives my tail a subtle little rub with her fingertips that tells me she'll make it up to me later.

"So you have cargo for us?" Mathiras asks, heading up the ramp toward the interior of the *Jabberwock*. "Or is this just a family reunion?"

"Both," Zoey says. She pinches my ass, then moves toward her brothers. Taking Kaspar by the arm, she leads the group into the ship. "You guys are staying for dinner—we're having chicken noodle soup. It's an Earth thing. Well...chicken equivalent, noodle equivalent soup. It's not exactly the same, but Fran's got it pretty close."

Adiron shoots me a look of fear and I just shrug. We've all had to endure the dinner parties where the females fix "human equivalents" of their foods and...they're not pleasing to mesakkah palates. But we endure it, because it makes Zoey happy to share these things with the other human females. She's not a fan of the food, but she likes trying them anyhow.

"And the cargo?" Kaspar asks his sister, as I fall in behind them, a few steps carefully *away from* Adiron.

"You'll never guess," Zoey says, shooting me a wicked look.

I smile back at my beautiful mate. I don't mind these visits with her family. Lately we've been scheduling our refueling stops to the same station that the *Little Sister* does so we can meet up for dinner and Zoey can catch up with her brothers. It always puts a brilliant smile on her lovely face, so I can endure Adiron's endless teasing.

How she tolerated him for ten years is amazing, because half the time I want to beat his head in. Of course, I suspect Adiron has that effect on everyone.

"Not more of those keffing worms, I hope," Kaspar says.

Zoey snickers.

Mathrias groans. "More inukni worms?"

"More," I agree. "There's been a high demand for them on the Outer Rim. Seems like food shipments are scarce and the locals are price gouging." I hate it. Zoey knows I hate it—it's one reason why we're offloading the worms to her brothers instead of taking them there ourselves. She knows I can't stand to see the starved, hopeful faces of the farmers as we arrive. They always hope we're a supply ship and all we've got are keffing worms.

Reminds me too much of my childhood.

"Almost sounds like someone should hijack a couple of supply ships and dump the cargo where it's most needed," Kaspar says casually.

Zoey's eyes light up. "If only we knew some pirates. Or two crews of them." She looks to me, hope in her expression.

A chance to work with her brothers and feed some hardworking people? The *Jabberwock's* got some time between our next contraband shipment. "We're in."

The only thing better than the happy squeal my mate lets out is the kiss she plants on me next. I haven't talked to Kivian and the others yet, but they'll come around. They know I'll do anything for Zoey.

I'd cross the entire universe for my female.

AUTHOR'S NOTE

Hello again!

I feel like I should start every author's note with a TADAA! Look at this thing I made! But I think that's because I'm excited to have you guys read it.

I loved writing this book. Loved, loved, loved. Sentorr was so very different from Zoey, and I adored pairing them up and watching them react. I also liked revisiting the *Fool*, and I'm a little sad that we're done with them.

Well, not DONE done, as I imagine that Zoey's brothers are going to pop up in my head at some point again, demanding their stories. For now, though, the focus will be on Ice Planet Barbarians and Fireblood Dragons until I catch up on those storylines. I've had to do a lot of schedule juggling this year and so those haven't gotten as much attention as I wanted and I miss them! Especially my barbarians. I'm trying to narrow my focus so there's not such huge gaps between where I'm taking stories in the future. I know several of you have been waiting anxiously to watch the Icehome storyline progress and I feel the same anxiety you do! We'll get there!

Until then, I hope you enjoy spending a little more time on the Dancing Fool. Excuse me, the Lovesick Fool...now the Jabberwock! Whatever they call themselves, I love this crew. Heck, I love all my characters, but some more than others. These definitely hold a special place in my heart.

<3 <3 <3

Ruby

PS — I didn't say what I'm working on next. That's because it's a project for my New York publisher and I'm focusing on it at the moment! Once it's in the can, I'll talk a little on Facebook about what's coming next, but most likely it'll be Icehome. We shall see!

THE CORSAIRS

Sexy blue space pirates and the human women they fall madly in love with!

THE CORSAIR'S CAPTIVE
Kivian, a too-slick alien pirate, meets his match in a scrappy human female.

IN THE CORSAIR'S BED
Tarekh's so ugly no female will ever want him, but it doesn't stop him from loving Catrin with everything he has.

ENTICED BY THE CORSAIR

Alyvos only feels settled when he's in a fight. But then he meets Iris and finds out that he's got so much more to live for...if only she can trust him.

WANT MORE?

For more information about upcoming books in the Ice Planet Barbarians, Fireblood Dragons, or any other books by Ruby Dixon, 'like' me on Facebook or subscribe to my new release newsletter.

Thanks for reading!

<3 Ruby

ALSO BY RUBY DIXON

FIREBLOOD DRAGONS

Fire in His Blood

Fire in His Kiss

Fire in His Embrace

Fire in His Fury

Fire In His Spirit

ICE PLANET BARBARIANS

Ice Planet Barbarians

Barbarian Alien

Barbarian Lover

Barbarian Mine

Ice Planet Holiday (novella)

Barbarian's Prize

Barbarian's Mate

Having the Barbarian's Baby (short story)

Ice Ice Babies (short story)

Barbarian's Touch

Calm(short story)

Barbarian's Taming

Aftershocks (short story)

Barbarian's Heart

Barbarian's Hope

Barbarian's Choice

Barbarian's Redemption

Barbarian's Lady

Barbarian's Rescue

Barbarian's Tease

The Barbarian Before Christmas (novella)

Barbarian's Beloved

ICEHOME

LAUREN'S BARBARIAN

VERONICA'S DRAGON

STAND ALONE

PRISON PLANET BARBARIAN

THE ALIEN'S MAIL-ORDER BRIDE

BEAUTY IN AUTUMN

THE KING'S SPINSTER BRIDE

THE ALIEN ASSASSIN'S CONVENIENT WIFE

BEDLAM BUTCHERS

Bedlam Butchers, Volumes 1-3: Off Limits, Packing Double, Double Trouble

Bedlam Butchers, Volumes 4-6: Double Down, Double or Nothing, Slow Ride

Double Dare You

BEAR BITES

SHIFT: Five Complete Novellas

INTRODUCTION

Redwoods inhabit and shape the environment of 450 miles of coastal California. This forest takes in more carbon dioxide per acre than any other on our planet, making it essential in controlling global warming.

As you observe these great trees throughout their range, you will notice a number of plants commonly sharing the shaded habitat they create.

Coast Redwoods and Western Sword Ferns

In the 'Cast of Characters' on pages 4-5, fifty of these plants have been arranged by bloom date, with successive plants usually flowering a bit later (depending on exposure, elevation, latitude, etc.) than the preceding ones. For each of the Redwood Community plants that make up the body of the book, there is an information page and a botanical print page for the reader to hand tint. To make this process possible, I removed the color, and adjusted the exposure, contrast and detail. Hand tinting was first used in the era before color photography to give life to black and white pictures. As you can see on the previous page, hand tinting allows the details of texture to show through. At the back of the book can be found a listing of botanical uses and plant family characteristics, pgs. 114-117, as well as a Glossary of the terms underlined in the text and an Index, pgs. 118-121.

2

PLACES FOR PRACTICE

You can find an interactive map of 40 Redwood parks to visit by searching on California Coastal Redwood Parks.

Here are two pictures of the Sword fern, one of the Coast Redwood's closest friends. Use them to practice on by adding a light green with your color pencils.

Cast of Characters

Bloom	Common Name	Scientific name	Page
Nov-Jan	Coast Redwood	*Sequoia sempervirens*	6
Dec-May	Calif. Milk Maids	*Cardamine californica*	8
Dec-Jun	Western Sword Fern	*Polystichum munitum*	10
Jan-Mar	Calif.Hazel	*Corylus cornuta*	12
Feb-Mar	Fetid Adder's Tongue	*Scoliopus bigelovii*	14
Feb-Apr	Common Horsetail	*Equisetum arvense*	16
Feb-Apr	Flowering Currant	*Ribes sanguinem*	18
Feb-Apr	Canyon Gooseberry	*Ribes menziesii*	20
Feb-Mar	False Soloman's Seal	*Maianthemum stellatum*	24
Feb-Apr	Western Trillium	*Trillium ovatum*	26
Feb-May	Miner's Lettuce	*Claytonia perfoliata*	28
Feb-May	Calif. Polypody Fern	*Polypodium californicum*	30
Feb-May	Calif. Bay	*Umbellularia californica*	32
Feb-May	Hound's Tongue	*Cynoglossum grande*	34
Feb-May	Giant Chain Fern	*Woodwardia fimbriata*	36
Feb-Jul	Calif. Sweet Grass	*Anthoxanthum occidentale*	38
Feb-Jul	Redwood Violet	*Viola sempervirens*	40
Feb-Jul	Wood Strawberry	*Fragaria vesca*	42
Feb-Aug	Redwood Sorrel	*Oxalis oregana*	44
Feb-Sep	Goldback Fern	*Pentagrama triangularis*	46
Mar-May	Wild Cucumber	*Marah oregana*	48
Mar-May	Madrone	*Arbutus menziesii*	50
Mar-May	Calif. Huckleberry	*Vaccinium ovatum*	52
Mar-Jun	Salmonberry	*Rubus spectablis*	54
Mar-Jun	Douglas Iris	*Iris douglasiana*	56

4